BODY BROKER

A Jack Dixon Novel
DANIEL M. FORD

sfwp.com

Library of Congress Cataloging-in-Publication Data
Names: Ford, Daniel M., 1978- author.
Title: Body broker : a Jack Dixon novel / Daniel M. Ford.
Description: Santa Fe, NE : Santa Fe Writer's Project, 2019. | Series: Jack Dixon
Identifiers: LCCN 2019009898 (print) | LCCN 2019012109 (ebook) |
    ISBN 9781733777704 (ebook) | ISBN 9781939650993 (paperback)
Subjects: | BISAC: FICTION / Mystery & Detective / Traditional British. |
    GSAFD: Mystery fiction.
Classification: LCC PS3606.O728 (ebook) | LCC PS3606.O728 B63 2019 (print) |
    DDC 813/.6--dc23
LC record available at https://lccn.loc.gov/2019009898

Published by SFWP
369 Montezuma Ave. #350
Santa Fe, NM 87501
(505) 428-9045
www.sfwp.com

Author's Note:

Jack Dixon inhabits an imagined world of violence and, in some cases, geography. Furnace Bay is a real geographical feature in Cecil County, Maryland, but not a real town. Neither is Farrington Academy a real school, nor reflective of any schools in the area.

Chapter 1

The first notes of "L.A. Freeway" pulled me out of sleep. I had the phone in my hand and was fumbling it to a stop before Guy Clark could start telling his wife to pack up the dishes. *Kind of a shitty division of labor*, I thought. "Man just sings about getting off the highway and his wife's got to do all the work. Figures."

Once I blinked my eyes clear I tapped the passcode into the phone. Two tries, after I fat-thumbed the first. Then I hauled myself to my feet, the deck pitching just a little under me, and flipped open my work email, which, surprisingly enough, had a couple messages in it.

One was the Under Secretary of the Department of Homeland Security requesting my assistance in the transfer of the money fund account in the amount of $5,750,000 into my bank as soon as I produced a routing number.

I flicked "report spam." The other was a furniture and home goods catalog trying desperately to sell me a dining room set. I looked at it with a bit of suppressed nesting-instinct-longing before tossing the phone on my unmade bed.

I could hear a few gulls, some people stomping around on the docks. I shuffled over to the fridge and looked inside.

A long-neglected can of Guinness, cold and seductive. Milk. One last jar of fancy almond butter sitting in front of a jar of plain, workmanlike organic peanut butter. Cocktail ingredients, neatly marshaled along the door. I grabbed the jar of almond butter and a tablespoon from the basket on top of the mini-fridge and walked topside while I had breakfast. I may have turned my alarm off but the song was in my head, and I murmured the chorus while I looked over the water.

"If I can just get off of this L.A. freeway without gettin' killed or caught…"

It was mid-September and the river was holding on to summer's heat, if not its humidity. The early morning sunlight—8:30 a.m. was early in my world—shimmered off the brown and gold water. A heron knifed into the shallows from the bank, then took off with a speared fish.

"Show off," I muttered, out of spite, as I chewed through a stubborn hunk of vanilla and whey-protein almond butter. I'd describe the flavor as "whey-protein forward." It had probably been shown a bottle of vanilla extract or a painting of a vanilla bean at some point in its manufacture.

I polished off the two remaining tablespoons in the jar, stuffed it into a plastic bag that served for garbage, and set about putting a gym bag together.

The marina was in a small riverside town, and full of recreational boats that were more often lovingly washed and cleaned up than they were taken out into the river or the Chesapeake Bay beyond. But there were usually people moving around it, starting a camping vacation, or heading to a bay island, loading folding bicycles and coolers in.

I lived here. Usually. For an extra few bucks a month in slip rent, the manager, a guy named Marty, let me hook up to the electric and the water. I gave him a hand with manual labor whenever he could catch me.

I kept a pretty close watch on Marty's comings and goings. Closer than he was able to keep on mine.

Coast looked clear, so I set out for the gym. It wasn't too long a walk from the marina to Pulaski Highway, then just a few minutes walking along the side of it like a hobo, in sweatpants and Converse.

I was about halfway there, starting to work up a sweat, when I heard the brief flare of a siren and the tell-tale sound of Interceptor wheels on gravel.

"Goddammit." I started to put my hands up when I heard a thick voice say, "Oh, for fuck's sake, Jack, get in the truck. We gotta talk."

I dropped my hands and turned around, taking in the Cecil County Sheriff's black SUV and the wall of blue-shirted deputy standing behind the open door.

"Jaysus, Bob," I sputtered, "you could've just called," I said as I scuffled along the gravel to his empty passenger side.

I slid in and he shut the doors, flicking the lights back on to merge back into traffic.

"I was driving to the marina to look for you," he said. Bob Sanderson—Corporal Sanderson—looked far too constrained by the driver's side of his car. "Manager told me you'd already taken off for the gym. Before nine a.m., too. Real dedication, getting out this early."

"Well, you know me. Rise early, shut the alarm off, have brunch, think real hard about the squat rack."

"Yeah. Look." Bob had something he wanted to tell me, that much I knew. The way his jaw clenched, the way his hands settled on the wheel. Something he wanted help with. I was eager; my last paycheck was dwindling fast and I needed work. But the key with a guy like Bob was giving him the space to figure out how to ask.

"Might be something you could look into."

Donut shortage? Run out of K-Cups and nobody in the station's got the IQ to operate a real coffee maker? Got to find your asshole and only have a map and a flashlight? Old lady's cheating on you again and you need to narrow the suspect pool down from the entire 7th Fleet?

Bob looked down at me. "No jokes?"

"Discretion seems like the better part of valor here, Bob. You could disappear me on the side of Route 40 and nobody'd know."

"Too much of you to disappear," he said, poking a finger disapprovingly into my arm, which was maybe not quite the sculpted rock Bob's was. But there are Greek marbles with a higher body fat percentage than him.

"Seriously. Got a lady looking for her son."

"That seems like the kind of thing the cops normally do," I said carefully.

"Yeah, it is, except this kid's not a minor. He just turned eighteen. Mom thinks he wasn't happy in school, wanted to drop out. Kinda looks like that's what's happened."

"Kid becomes an adult, takes off, not a crime, so…"

"Not my circus. Mom's desperate to find him, doesn't seem to have a clue how to start."

"Dad?"

"Didn't talk to him. Doesn't seem to be in the picture."

"First place to look then," I said.

"See? You're already developing theories." By now, the SUV had pulled up in front of Waterfront Fitness. In the front window, a bevy of Lululemon and Under Armour-clad folks worked diligently and miserably on the treadmills and ellipticals. "Where do you want to meet her?"

"I suppose my home office is out?"

"I ain't sending her to the marina."

"Coffee shop, then."

"Which one?"

"The one closest to the marina, whichever that is. I haven't got endless money for Lyft."

"Jesus, Jack. You gotta be the only PI ain't got a car."

"It's an aesthetic."

"A what?"

"I can't afford one, Bob."

"Give up the boat and you'll have the money."

"Death first," I said. "What's the lady's name?"

"Susan Kennelly. I'll text you her info," he said, slipping his cell out of his pocket.

"I thought Maryland was cracking down on hand-held cell phone use while operating a vehicle."

Bob glared at me while he thumbed at his phone, which looked comically tiny in his oversized hand. "One p.m.?"

I nodded as I felt my phone buzz in my pocket. I popped open the door and swung halfway out of it. "I appreciate you sending work my way. If I can help her I will."

"That's why I came looking for you. Now go try and do a real workout, huh?"

"Only because you inspire me, Bob." I shut the door, adjusted the gym bag on my shoulder, and shuffled reluctantly into the gym.

Chapter 2

Waterfront Fitness was a lie. It wasn't on the waterfront; it wasn't within a half-mile of the water in any direction. But it had its advantages. Walking distance from the marina. Twenty-five dollars a month for 24-hour service meant I could afford it and it worked with my hours.

Lastly, and most importantly, all of the regular staff had long since given up on trying to talk to me.

Or at least I'd thought so.

I spotted a disgustingly slim-hipped, close-bearded, hair-gelled new kid in a tight orange staff shirt walking directly into my path.

"Hey, Mr. Dixon," he said, extending a hand. "I'm Nick. The other staff told me to make sure to introduce myself to you, ask if you needed any help or a check-up on your form or…"

I resisted, with an effort of will that could well have been called heroic, the urge to take his proffered hand and squeeze it a little too hard. He was wearing a big class ring with a glittering blue stone. It would've hurt like hell.

I did not like it when pleasantries and small talk stood between me and my workout.

Instead I gritted my back teeth and shook his hand. "I'm good."

"Are you sure? How about I just check out your form for a minute? Mr. Vachess was really insistent that I try to talk with you."

I'm the hazing ritual for the new kid. Okay then. Let's haze.

I brushed past him and went up to the squat racks, the gloriously empty squat racks.

I am one of perhaps a dozen clients of Waterfront Fitness who come there to use the squat racks. I never have to wait. Another reason I loved it here.

I adjusted the height; I like it pretty low so I've really got to get under it. Plus, the kid had the audacity to be a solid three inches taller than me. Then, looking Nick dead in the eye, I put two plates on either side of the bar. I got under it, backed out, and banged out five reps that all fell somewhere on a rising spectrum of mediocrity, barely getting parallel. When I'd racked it, I looked at Nick and said, "Maybe you could give me some form pointers."

"No problem, Mr. Dixon."

He expertly settled under the bar, lifted it clear, and slowly went down into a perfect below-parallel squat, chattering about the width of my stance and where to point my feet and the importance of keeping the abdominal muscles activated. Five more reps followed, and for all the effort he showed the bar might as well have been made of plastic. All the while he chattered about placement of the feet, how I held the bar too high on my back, and other shit I didn't listen to.

* * *

Two hours later, I wasn't sure who hazed whom. Nick was not, in fact, the reedy-legged poseur I'd taken him to be. Well, reedy-legged, maybe, but I couldn't find a way to slow him down. Little bastard just about did my legs in on the squats. Then he followed me all over the joint. I finally bested him on the deadlift, where I was certainly lifting twice his bodyweight. My legs were letting me know it, but I'd always felt that a workout wasn't over if I didn't want to collapse.

I almost *did* collapse in the shower, and took my time getting dressed. I had a little time on my hands so I pondered walking back to the marina, but that would waste the shower and the primping I'd done. So I thumbed open the phone, ordered up a ride, and awaited it in the parking lot.

Sure enough, in a few moments a silver Corolla rolled up and bore me a few miles to a shopping center in air-conditioned comfort. I checked the time on my phone: 12:15.

"Well," I said after I tipped my driver, "here's hoping I don't alienate the staff enough to get kicked out."

I went in, dumped my bag on a table right in front of an outlet, ordered coffee, and settled in.

I pulled a tablet from my gym bag—I always bring it, in case the spirit moves me to mount a treadmill at the gym. As much as I wanted to open a book and grab some reading time, I decided to do just the tiniest bit of quick snooping on Susan Kennelly.

* * *

By the time I was done my second cup of coffee and pondering the lunch options—which is to say, pondering the salads, because I have a policy of avoiding joy at lunch—I knew that Susan Kennelly used "Ms" but had kept her husband's last name. I had looked at her divorce records—five years ago, with full custody to her, which seemed largely uncontested. Irregular visitation with the dad, whose name was Tom. Only the one kid, Gabriel, who had turned eighteen just a week prior.

I was able to look at most of Ms. Kennelly's Facebook page. Lots of vaguely spiritual memes, photos of Thanksgiving centerpieces, Jack-o-Lanterns, and Christmas trees of years past. A few of her kid. He was the athletic type; hard to tell how tall he was, but he had young man's muscle on his frame. Dressed nicely in the photos, some in a school uniform, complete with crested blazer. Even outside of that, polo shirts, khakis, sharp jeans, belts, that kind of thing. Clean-shaven, no visible jewelry, looking directly at the camera and occasionally even smiling. A couple of him in a track or cross-country uniform in mid-stride.

I had just about talked myself into ordering a chicken Caesar, hold the croutons, dressing on the side, when my phone buzzed with a text from the number Bob had given me. I slapped the case closed on my tablet and looked to the entrance of the store.

A woman, a few years older than me but bearing them well, neat bobbed hair, flat shoes. She was dressed in anticipation of the season rather than for the weather, in the way so many people around here are: a light blue scarf draped around her neck, jeans, boots, a half-sleeve sweater, Vera Bradley bag.

I stood up and offered her a low-key wave, suddenly feeling underdressed in a blue-and-white raglan, khaki shorts, and bright blue-and-neon green running shoes.

"Mr. Dixon?"

"Yes, ma'am," I said as I pushed out a chair for her. She extended her hand and I took it, carefully, while she introduced herself. Her palm was a bit clammy, but her handshake wasn't limp. I stood, waiting for her to sit, which she didn't, so we both awkwardly stood for a while.

"Oh," she said, with a nervous laugh, before she finally sat. "You're being a gentleman."

"Only just." I sat back down, back straight, feet resting on the legs of the chair. "Can I get you anything? Coffee?"

She shook her head, clasped her hands on the table, and looked at me again.

"You're not what I was expecting."

"I get that a lot."

"I suppose I was thinking, you know…a detective. In a suit with a gun on his belt And…maybe a hat?"

"Well, I didn't expect to be meeting any potential clients today."

She nodded, tapping her wrists on the table. "You work independently, or…?"

"As much as possible. Technically, I'm an employee of the Dent-Clark Agency but they allow me a lot of latitude to operate independently." I chose the words carefully; they were as many syllables as I'd said to other people in the last three days combined, I think.

When I wasn't working I didn't get out much, and the places I did go, folks generally didn't talk to me.

"Before I start, how much did Bob tell you?"

"Corporal Sanderson only told me that you were worried about someone," I said, dropping my voice a bit. Clients typically wanted to be discreet.

She nodded. "Yes…would you mind, maybe…telling me a little. About your experience."

"I'm licensed in the state," I said, "and I can show you my license if you'd like. I've been with Dent-Clark for two years and change."

"And before that, you were a cop, Bob told me?"

I nodded. "For a couple of years, yes. I was with the Department of Natural Resources Marine Police."

"Two years here, two years there…you're not one of those sorts who has to quit and start over every so often, are you?"

"I'd like to think not, ma'am."

"You were military, maybe…keep calling me ma'am, sit up straight." She pointed a finger at me. "One of those special forces types, I bet…that's the beard and the loner thing."

I shook my head gently. "You're halfway right, Ms. Kennelly. I was in the Navy, but the closest I ever got to any SEALs, or any other special forces types, was when I was slopping food on their tray." I cleared my throat and resettled on the chair. "This isn't getting us any closer to what I can help you with."

"Yes. Well…my son. Gabriel." She paused, pressed her lips together. "How much did Bob tell you?"

"Corporal Sanderson said your son hadn't had any contact with you in a couple of days. I assume this is unusual behavior, and that you haven't been able to locate him."

She nodded, sharply, and I had the sense she was only just holding herself together.

"Ms. Kennelly, would you like to leave here, talk somewhere more private?"

"Where?"

I hadn't thought that far ahead.

"Presumably you have a car. You might feel a little less conspicuous in it."

She nodded. I stood, waited for her, then followed her out into the parking lot. She led me to a Honda Pilot, dark green, pretty much standard issue for the suburbs around here. I noted the political bumper-stickers on the back, a school sticker with the same crest as her son's blazer: Farrington Academy.

The car was scrupulously clean, not even coffee cups in the cupholders. I slid into the passenger seat, holding myself carefully, hands on my lap, trying to stay as far away from her as I could within the confines of the front seat. I didn't want to give her the slightest reason to feel fearful.

"Where were we," I ventured as she gripped the steering wheel.

"My son hasn't called or picked up his phone for three days. I called his school…it's a boarding school, you know. They said he had gotten a sick note for the past two days. This morning he was not in class and he had not gone to the infirmary. When they checked his room, they found all the necessary drop-out paperwork, filled out, signed, notarized on his desk."

I held back a sigh. It was looking like I might have to speak some unpleasant truths to Susan Kennelly.

"And as he is eighteen, he doesn't need your permission, does he?"

She shook her head, and I saw her jaw quiver. Tears were on the verge. I carefully slipped a clean white handkerchief out of a pocket and held it out to her.

"It's clean," I said. She took it, unfolded one corner, and dabbed at her eyes. "Now, Ms. Kennelly, Corporal Sanderson will probably have already told you, that Gabriel being eighteen, if he has simply disappeared, no crime has necessarily been committed."

"I know," she said, "that's exactly what the police told me, in a lot of roundabout ways of saying they couldn't help yet unless there was something else to it. Are you telling me the same thing?"

"Not at all. If you want to hire me to find Gabriel, I will make every possible effort to do so, and I will share my findings with you. But what I can't do is promise to bring him home."

"Why not?"

"Because if he's gone somewhere of his own volition, conking him over the head and bundling him home *would* be a crime."

She laughed, slightly. More tears, a little careful sniffling. I wasn't getting my handkerchief back, but that's why I carried two.

"I don't think you'd need to conk him on the head. You look like you could probably just pick him up and carry him home."

I grinned, very faintly. "I'd have to catch him first, Ms. Kennelly. And that seems unlikely. I'm not fleet of foot." She laughed a little bit more.

"So will you...do whatever it is you do?"

"You'll have to call Dent-Clark and officially hire me. They'll take care of those details." I slipped a card from a slim metal case in the same pocket the handkerchief had come from and handed it over.

"Then I would ask you to email me a list of some information. Address is on the card." I took a small metal-sided notebook from a pocket of my gym bag, slipped the pen out of the slot on its side. Carefully I wrote up a list: Father's contact info. Contact person at the school. Close friends/close friend's parents. Significant others/ parents. Any local relations (aunts, uncles, cousins). By the time I was done the list ran to three pages, but they were small pages, and my printing was crisp. I might even be tempted to call it copperplate. I resisted the urge to either admire it or point out just how neat and regular it was to Ms. Kennelly. Sometimes doing a thing well had to be its own reward.

"And then, what'll you do?"

"I'll start running down these contacts. Probably the school first, or his father."

"Good luck with that one," she said, with a snort.

"Hard to get hold of?"

"He hasn't answered any of my calls. Or emails. Or texts. He normally doesn't, but I thought hearing that his son was missing might move him slightly."

"He local?"

"Wilmington," she said. "Old money."

"Well," I said, "I'll wear a suit. For both."

She nodded, took the papers, and carefully put them inside a pocket of her bag. "When will you start?"

"As soon as the office tells me you've hired me; this is a matter of protecting myself and the firm legally. I can start to do some prep work and research, of course, but I can't go talking to anyone and pressing your interests until you're officially a client."

"You're very precise about things. Is that a military-man thing?"

"It could be, ma'am. It helps to make sure that everyone knows what they can expect of me."

She looked at the business card, which she'd left on the dash. "So I just call them?"

I nodded again. "Should I get out so I can begin preparing?"

She nodded. I opened the door. She said quickly, "How often are missing kids found? Don't tell me if it's something awful, like five percent. It is, isn't it?"

"A lot better than that. More like eighty percent. Varies depending on how you define missing and kid…but chances are good that we'll find him."

She nodded and I set off across the parking lot, closing the door to her SUV carefully. I settled the gym bag where I liked it and decided I might as well walk. The afternoon was getting a little cooler, with a breeze coming off the water.

I wasn't even halfway there when my phone buzzed in my pocket, and I knew who it was before I even thumbed it open. I didn't *want* to talk to my boss; who does? But it wasn't wise to avoid him.

"Dixon," I said as I slid the earbud in and let the mic dangle against my beard.

"Jack, are you talking to me while walking on the side of Route 40?"

"That is the way back to the marina, Jason."

"Or you could join the prior century and buy a car."

"I'm trying to minimize my carbon footprint."

"Bullshit. Your boat's got to be at least as bad as some little econobox with wheels. It's just part of your…thing."

"What thing is that?"

"Oh, I dunno. Some old-timey romantic hero, Hemingway-man-of-the-sea bullshit. But hey, you've got a client."

"Good to know. I don't think it ought to be too difficult. Kid likely ran off somewhere he knows—dad, a girlfriend, a boyfriend, a party house."

"Don't let your keen investigative insight get in the way of gathering facts. Lots of facts."

I didn't like the way his voice sounded. Like a card-sharp who sees an easy mark. A little hungry, a little eager.

"Her credit's good?"

"Oh, very good. She paid a retainer. Didn't even try to negotiate."

I suddenly found myself wondering why Susan Kennelly drove a Honda Pilot instead of something more like an Escalade or a GLC.

"Well, I'm not gonna just bilk the woman, Jason. If I stumble across her kid between here and my boat I'm closing the case."

"You white knight, you. Never could see the potential of the expense account."

I liked Jason enough to believe he was half-joking. Maybe only half, because a man's got a business to run, and a whale is a whale. Also he hadn't done the face-to-face; harder to reduce someone to their FICO score when you've done that. He went on.

"Look, I've got a little…feeling about this one."

"Don't say it."

"My Spidey-Sense is tinglin' a little. Maybe just a little. Seems real strange."

"I got a dinner says I find the kid drunk with a romantic partner or having signed some enlistment papers."

"Where at?"

"Prost."

"You're on," Jason said. "Go get your suit out of storage," he said. I heard his fingers clicking over a keyboard. "You're gonna need it to visit Farrington. Not to mention the father."

"It's not in storage. It's in my closet."

"Then get it to a damn dry cleaner and pay them extra to hurry it up. Muscled-up Parrothead isn't gonna play with the Old Money."

"That is the single most insulting thing you've ever said to me. I'm tempted to rescind our wager."

"But we both know you wouldn't, even if I wasn't your boss. You said it, now you have to do it. All part of your bullshit."

"Is all that typing I hear because Ms. Kennelly's already forwarded the list of contacts?" Classic misdirection.

"Yep. You're gonna have to come by and take a company car. First thing tomorrow morning."

"Define first thing."

"Office opens at eight a.m. sharp."

"You're a cruel man, Clark."

"That's *Mister* Clark."

"If I need to be there at eight, best you task an incoming drone to stop for me. Ride-sharing's too unpredictable."

"Fine. But be ready by seven-thirty."

"You're history's greatest…" But before I could finish, the dead silence made it clear that the call had ended. I slipped the phone away and continued my hike.

Chapter 3

People who hear I have a '68 Thunderbird are usually *really* disappointed when I show them pictures of a 34-foot houseboat instead of a car. But the car, no matter how pretty to look at, doesn't have the amenities the *Belle of Joppa* does. It's not large, as houseboats go. But it suits me. My bunk, my galley, my portable bar — an old packing case I'd converted with the use of my best friend's garage full of tools — some boxes of books and clothes.

Unfortunately, cable is not part of the houseboat package I negotiated with Marty, so I sat on the deck that afternoon, siphoning wifi from a restaurant upriver just a bit. I started with the school. Farrington Academy overlooked the nearby town of Furnace Bay like some kind of colonial fort. Some of the architecture even suggested fortification rather than educational institute.

I glanced at the history of the place. Apparently the founder had come from a military family; grandfather a Continental Army captain, father a lieutenant in 1812, and himself a colonel of Union artillery. Family got rich from the noble art of blowing their fellow man to hell, I guess. Rich enough for Colonel Farrington to found this school in the late 1870s, committing the bulk of his fortune to it.

And apparently now it asked families to commit the bulk of *their* fortunes so little Tylers and Kierstins can have the benefit of the Colonel's educational vision. Seems it was a day and a boarding school and based on what Ms. Kennelly had told me, Gabriel'd been a boarder. The whole ticket looked to come in north of fifty grand a year, which was a number so vast as a price for *high school* that I had to sit in stunned silence for a moment. It was much like the regular silence that already reigned on the *Belle*, aside from the lapping river and the occasional bird, only with my mouth slightly open and my eyes lifted just over the horizon.

I considered venturing inside to the galley to make myself a restorative cocktail, but it was not quite three, and a Monday. I'd found that opening up the bar this soon on the first day of the workweek was not precisely a formula for investigative excellence. Heroically, I centered myself and soldiered on.

The current headmaster was a Dr. Elijah Marks. Judging by his photo on the school website he had come straight from central casting: stylishly graying beard, gold-rimmed spectacles, and what I expected to be positively dangerous levels of tweed.

If I had the opportunity to meet Dr. Marks, and he wasn't wearing a waistcoat with a watch-chain and a Phi Beta Kappa key, I'd be sorely disappointed.

"Okay, Clark," I muttered spitefully. "You were right. I am gonna need the suit."

Houseboat living does not come with an abundance of storage space, but I did keep the suit in a bag, and hanging in a place of, if not honor, at least recognition of its practical value. A suit could open more doors than a Henley and a pair of jeans, it's true. I unzipped a bit of the JC Penny bag—light gray, a little darker gray piping on the lapels. I sniffed; all seemed well. No obvious wrinkles, so I zipped it back up and put it back in a more prominent place where I'd see it when I woke up. Then I went back to my illicit wifi.

The school seemed easy enough. The usual *yes* and *no, sir* or *ma'am* that I defaulted to anyway would do the job just fine. The father was proving a bit harder to run down. I didn't get anything usable on his name, so I started looking at the big Wilmington firms, scanning the pages of their top employees. I was striking out looking for any Kennellys, though. Someone had been paying the freight at Farrington and I doubted it was the mom. Could've been a rich grandparent lurking behind all of it.

On a whim, I surfed back to the Farrington page and looked for notable alumni. I *did* find a Kennelly or two but they were far older than Gabriel's father should've been. One had graduated in 1908 and, apparently, gone on to war profiteering in a chemicals and mining firm.

That's not what the website's bio said, mind you, but possessing a keen investigative instinct I could read between the lines of "pioneered industrial and military chemical solutions" to find "created new ways to blow people up or made the old ways more efficient."

I went ahead and looked up this M.W. Kennelly. You knew a man was Someone when he went by his initials, or so I told myself. He had shuffled off the mortal coil in 1972, but had passed on considerable wealth to just two children, both the product of a late-in-life marriage. Neither of them rated their own Wikipedia pages, but it was certainly likely that one of them was Gabriel's grandfather.

On an impulse I dialed up the Farrington number. Midway through the second ring, a crisp, professional woman's voice answered.

"Farrington Academy, Amy Riordan speaking, how may I help you?"

"Hello, Ms. Riordan," I began. "My name's Jack Dixon. I'm with the Dent-Clark firm," I said. When put that way, most folks assume it's a law office rather an investigation agency. That sometimes opens a few more doors. "I've been retained by a Farrington parent. I was hoping I could schedule an appointment this week to speak to some people."

"Is this a legal matter?"

"Not in the way you probably mean, ma'am," I said. "I am not a lawyer or a law enforcement officer. I'm an investigator. It's about a recent drop-out."

She sighed lightly. "Gabriel?"

"Kennelly, yes, ma'am."

Another sigh. Amy Riordan had thoughts on Gabriel Kennelly's dropping out. I reached for my notebook and scribbled her name down on it with _ask_ underlined several times.

"Could you hold for a moment, Mr. Dixon?"

"Of course." Music buzzed into the phone. Thirty seconds of droning strings playing some unrecognizable classical thing. The part of me that wished I knew things strained to identify it.

"Mr. Dixon?"

"Yes, ma'am."

"Would 2:30 tomorrow with the Dean of Student Life suit? He's probably best suited to fill you in on any details regarding Gabriel's life at Farrington, as well as his social circle."

"That would be great, ma'am. I'll see you tomorrow afternoon."

"Please look for the visitor parking signs," she said. "When you buzz at the front door, be prepared to present your ID and license."

"Will do," I said, scratching _parking_ and _buzz/license_ into the notepad.

"Thank you, Mr. Dixon." She hung up. I set the phone down and did my best to picture Amy Riordan but the best I could come up with were the women who staffed the desks at every school I ever attended. The kind of women that the word "stolid" was hanging around waiting to apply to. They knew everyone, held every secret close to be judiciously meted out, knew which kids were genuinely good and which could fake it, and had a lid on every potential crisis before it could break out. They had candy in their desks, but only the terrible kinds, like individually wrapped butterscotches of ancient provenance, dusty mints, things that you thought were going to be chocolate but never were. It would pay to get Amy Riordan on my side; I could tell that much. But I had a strong suspicion she'd be immune to my charm, even at its most devastating settings.

I set the phone down and looked over my notes. A missing puzzle piece here was the father. The internet was positively bereft of meaningful references to a Tom Kennelly in Wilmington, as an alumnus of Farrington, or anything the hell else.

I decided to put dad on the back burner. I typed up an email to my boss summarizing my contact with the school and plan of action. Nothing to do at that point but stretch out on the top deck with a book, which I did, until I switched on a radio to listen to the Orioles game. The wildcard hunt was a distant memory and a late season series against Toronto did not do much to fire the imagination. But there were worse ways to while away the evening than to listen to Joe Angel's voice float over the water. Once the third inning came along I decided to open the bar, and mixed up a Manhattan: Ravenwood Rye, orange bitters, a suggestion of vermouth, a squeeze of blood orange juice I had made the week before.

I sat and thought about the case, such as it was. The high likelihood was that Gabriel Kennelly had made an impulsive decision — for a friend, a girl or a guy — and hadn't gone far. I sipped my cocktail, listened to the water lap at the hull of the *Belle*, and thought of easy money, fall breezes, and the next Orioles playoff run.

Chapter 4

They don't make off-the-rack suits in my size. They just don't. A 48 or 50 jacket will leave my shoulders comfortable and flap like a loose sail around my waist. And for some reason they think every guy with larger shoulders is going to have long legs. Let's just say that on my budget, I don't make a suit look as good as it ought to.

Nevertheless, I was in the parking lot of the marina in my gray suit, robin's-egg blue shirt, silver tie and matching pocket square, black shoes, black belt, looking like the world's most overdressed hitchhiker.

Soon enough a car slowed down. I suppressed a groan. *Clark, you son of a bitch.*

It was a small gray Volvo, with bits of orange kit peeking out here and there, a loud exhaust, a spoiler, and some other dumb bullshit involved. Its owner could and would tell you all about the tires, the performance kit on the engine, and the color of the paint — probably Matte Phantom Mist, and he only chose that because he couldn't get it in camo.

The dumbest bullshit of all was behind the wheel. Brock Diamante, the newest hire and biggest pain in the ass in Dent-Clark investigations, straight out of the Army. High and tight haircut, a t-shirt with some kind of operator patch on the chest, cargo pants bloused over black combat boots. The back of the car was filled with pointless tactical gear, but at least it was boxed up. I wasn't super thrilled with the Glock riding his right hip, but there sure wasn't anything to do about it besides grin and bear it. It was a short drive to the main office.

Music blared through the windows. Some awful combination of over-produced guitar and twanged vocals spat at high velocity.

I popped open the passenger door and slid into the seat while he revved the engine. At least he kept his ride clean—if it had been almost any other employee picking me up, I'd have had a couple of weeks' worth of Wawa wrappers and breakfast sandwich boxes to sweep aside in order to sit down.

As I got in, he turned the music down to a barely eardrum-shattering level and handed over a steaming Wawa cup.

"Thanks for the coffee," I said.

"Boss said I had to. Also said you'd want these." He dropped a handful of yellow sweetener packets into my open palm. With practiced care, I eased the top off, ripped the packets open with my teeth two at a time, and dumped them in.

"Don't know why you need coffee that sweet," he said with slight derision, nudging his music back up.

"It's the only sweet thing I consume," I said through clenched teeth as I ripped open another. Once I had it all squared away, I pointedly turned the radio down.

Brock glared at me but didn't reach for the dial. "What you got against this stuff, man? Country Rap is…"

"It's cultural appropriation, first of all," I said. "And it sounds like someone shitting in my ear."

"Sorry it ain't have enough washtub bass and jug-blowing for ya," he muttered.

I let that pass, sipped the coffee. At least the kid had done that.

"What you coming into the office for?" he ventured.

"Boss said I had to," I murmured.

"I mean what are you working on?"

"I know what you meant," I said. "But I'm not entirely sure what I'm working on yet."

"Anything important?"

"All cases are important, Brock."

"Well I'm tired of parking outside every Motel Hotsheets between here and Aberdeen on Route 40 trying to snap pictures of a husband looking for some strange. I figure if Clark is making you come into the office, it's gotta be for something interesting."

"Wandering kid."

"That's cop work."

"Kid is a relative term. He's legally an adult but this is abnormal behavior, so a pal in the sheriff's office referred the client to me."

Brock chewed on his lip a while. "You gonna need a partner or…"

"No," I said.

"Man, why does the boss let you work alone? Nobody else gets to do that."

"Best ask him," I said, taking another sip of my coffee. Whatever the Bullshit Volvo had under the hood, Brock definitely got a lot out of it. We were passing everything on 40. I glanced at the needle.

"County sees you going 88, you're paying a hefty fine."

"Not if I got a friend of the sheriff sitting next to me."

"Never met the sheriff," I said.

"Whatever." He got sullen, turned his music back up, and I listened to rap about trucks and shotguns and blonde girls in overalls for the remainder of the ride.

The offices of Dent-Clark are, on the outside, about as nondescript as you can imagine. Just another frontage in an office park near the Delaware state line, a discreet sign, unobtrusive cameras everywhere. Brock backed into a parking space with the requisite élan his generation seemed to find so important.

"Thanks for the ride," I said, stepping out of the car. He hustled into work with a little backwards wave at me. I took my time, buttoning my suit jacket, which necessitated sucking in my gut a little more than I would've liked to admit. I checked the fold of my square and stepped smartly in.

Chapter 5

Inside, Dent-Clark was everything the modern investigative professional could've wanted. Sure, it was a cube farm, but it was a cube farm with tech. More cloud computing power than any of us knew what to do with, latest generation Mac desktops, MacBook airs, iPads, and every third cube featuring a large touchscreen to which anybody in the nearby pod could send documents, photos, any pertinent info, so that colleagues could work together in a realm of perfect information sharing.

I saw the heads of early-arrivers peeking up above cube walls staring at me. I refused to meet any of their gazes as I walked past each pod on my way to the management corridor. I was an oddity, an employee of the firm who was almost never in the office, and *definitely* never in a suit.

I put on confident smile number two—not fully arrogant, hardly subdued—and walked on.

Jason's office door was half open, so I gave it a slight knock and slid in. A big man—bigger than me. Dressed well, like he was every day. French cuffs, cufflinks that matched the tie bar, silver with some kind of simple blue stone. White shirt, blue tie, braces, suit jacket on a hanger on a hook by the wall. Two monitors on his desk, a typewriter on a desk to the side because he wanted us to think he could be old school.

There were two safes against the back wall, one for receipts, cash, valuables we might be holding onto. The other held company firearms. Jason rose to greet me, coming around his desk and extending a hand. His beard was shorter and better clipped than mine, and he wore his suit more naturally, even with suspenders. We shook hands.

"Jack," he said. "I should make you clean up and come in every day."

I grinned and kept shaking his hand. "If my appointment with the school is at 2:30, why am I here at eight in the morning?"

"Because there's other legwork to do. The father, an uncle. Work them, widen the circle, find the family friends."

"Father's a problem. Not having a lot of luck pinning him down."

"Which is why you're lucky you work for me," said Jason. "Father is an executive vice president of something called ADI Holdings."

I felt a tinge of wounded pride. Maybe even something resembling professional disappointment. I muted it. "I spent a couple hours yesterday trying to find him, where he worked. Got nothing."

"How exactly did you use that time?"

"Well, I traced out as much of the family as I could. Far as I can tell, the great-grandfather graduated from Farrington, invented some new way to bomb people, or to disperse lethal chemicals via artillery, or…"

"Don't need a history lesson."

"Look, the best I could do is find that there were two brothers, Oscar and Tom, and given what else I knew about the family tree, both of them were probably loaded."

"Did you, at any point, *ask the mother* where her ex-husband worked?"

Silence.

"I did not."

"Let me take a crack at this." Jason went back behind his desk and sat in his executive chair. I estimated it cost as much as all of the clothing I owned combined. "You didn't want to appear insensitive, so you didn't ask Ms. Kennelly this basic question when you talked to her. What's more, because you're *you*, you wanted to appear all-knowing, and come up with your list of contacts, build out the circle all on your lonesome."

"That, uh, is about right."

He tapped a few keys on the wireless keyboard before him, its keys glowing red. My phone buzzed in my shirt pocket.

"There's his contact info. Office is in Wilmington. My guess is you're going to find a single bank of offices in a nondescript office park, a PO box, a couple of secretaries and a whole lot of executives who spend more time on the Acela and the golf course than they do in Delaware."

"So I'm going to Wilmington first."

"Sure are."

"If I disappear into the void of encroaching corporate hegemony, what'll you do without me?"

"Hire an investigator who is slightly less of a pain in the ass and comes into the office of his own volition." Jason wandered over to the safe — the weapons safe — and began spinning one of the dials.

"I'm not carrying a gun into a *school*," I said.

"The cars have lockboxes for them," he said as the dial opened a panel. He pressed his thumb on it, and locking cylinders disengaged. "And you're the one worried about encroaching corporate hegemony."

"And if I leave it in the car and park in the wrong spot, you just gave a tow-truck guy a company registered piece."

"If the tow truck guy can open the lockbox, he deserves to have it."

"Clark," I said, digging my heels in. "I'm not carrying a firearm. Not today. This is normal walking around bullshit. Besides, I don't know if our licenses are good in Delaware."

"There and PA and I'm working on Virginia," he said. "You can have your way this time. But don't come crying to me when somebody doesn't take you seriously because you haven't got this on your hip." He slipped the pistol he'd been about to set on his desk back into the locker and removed something else. "Here." He set down a different holstered weapon, the bright yellow plastic construction proclaiming its nonlethal punch.

"Christ," I said. "The X2? You know how many people those've killed?"

"So long as you don't paint any skulls on this one, I don't care. Put it on."

I grumbled, but stepping down from a surely lethal firearm to an at least probably-not-lethal Taser was far as I was likely to get. I clipped it on to my belt, and arranged it so it sat on my right hip.

"Anything else? Some body armor? Sniper rifle in the trunk? Maybe I can mount a Ma Deuce on the hood…"

"Of a Nissan? Come on. The hood wouldn't hold up to anything heavier than a BAR."

"Well I'll see if I can find one at the next antique show. Am I leaving now?"

"Nah. If he was some kind of hedge fund goon you could bet he'd be hard at his desk by eight a.m. But this smells like the kind of sinecure wealth minus ambition can land you. Not likely in the office till ten. Go outside, grab a workstation, start a file."

"Looping anyone in?"

"Me and Diamante."

"Really? Diamante?"

"I'm not asking you to take him with you. Just show him how a case file is built. He's got a lot of gifts but he's a little weak on investigational procedure."

"Fine, fine. We done?"

"Yep. Got an hour. Start the clock."

I opened my phone and clicked on our billing and reportage app. The case was already listed. I opened it up, started a billing clock, selecting "Research and Coordination" as the activity, and went out to find an empty cube.

Chapter 6

I slid my coat around an office chair with a wire back, flicked the mouse of the desktop into wakefulness, and set about doing some work. We had some kind of software—I didn't pay attention to what it was called, only how it worked—that made this kind of thing a breeze. A few clicks on drop-down menus and I had a "Case File—Kennelly, Gabriel" opened, with tags MISSING and DROP-OUT as well as geographical tags for ELKTON, WILMINGTON, FARRINGTON, and FURNACE BAY. I shared it to Clark and Diamante, giving editing powers only to the former. Then I started filling in contacts. We had places for all of it: immediate family, secondary family, classmates, coworkers, teachers. I filled in as much as I had, including phone numbers, addresses, brief descriptors, and so on. I put in the appointment I had at the school, my contact person there.

I took another moment to ponder just what I might find at the school. Dour, sober, serious teachers, I had no doubt. Workmen and women of the classroom, building ponderous edifices of learning in the fragile and moldable minds of the cream of the tri-state area.

Much as I might grumble about coming into the office, it felt good to do this kind of work. I might like to imagine that I'd crack every case brought to me by simply sitting on the deck of the *Belle*, whiskey in hand, and think my way clear to the solution. But more often than not it was this — laying out every piece of info you had, where your eyes and others could see it — that led where you needed to go.

It was quick, easy work, but satisfying in its way, and it killed an hour before I had to get in a car and drive to Wilmington.

I paused at the key rack at the front of the office. Company cars had company key-rings, and there were four available, three had Nissan keys, and one had a Ford key. The Mustang was free.

But Jason had clearly said Nissan. I knew what I could push and how far; this would've been over that line.

Five minutes later I was tooling up I-95 in a late model Sentra.

Chapter 7

I think that if there were a "Boring Highway, Suburban Division" contest, the stretch of I-95 from Cecil County on up to Wilmington, Delaware would win going away. Marshlands compete with nondescript roadside woods and the occasional industrial hellscape. The only brief relief is passing the Riverfront and the minor league baseball stadium. I like seeing a baseball stadium in a city; makes it feel more approachable.

Pulling off onto Market Street in Wilmington was practically a relief. My phone was bleating at me that my destination was nearby, so I pulled into the nearest parking lot, took my ticket, nabbed the first spot, and got out. I started adjusting the Taser on my belt, then thought better of it entirely. I unlocked the car, slipped the damn thing off, and stuck it in the lockbox bolted into the frame under the dashboard, and straightened the line of my suit.

I didn't like carrying a weapon, not even a nonlethal one, and nothing about the job today should've required it. I hit the pavement.

So far, my boss' guess at what I was likely to find was spot-on but for one thing. The office wasn't nondescript. It was in one of the tallest buildings downtown.

I pulled out my phone and busied myself doing nothing while I stood just aside from the entrance. What I was really doing was looking up through my eyebrows at the layout. Looked like a security desk, with one guard sitting behind a bank of monitors. No detector.

The guard did not impress me as possessing a righteous zeal for justice and peace. His belly strained the buttons of his gray uniform and he appeared absorbed in something on the desk, given the way the interior lights reflected off the dome of his head.

Act like you belong somewhere and damn few people in this world will question it. Holding my phone forward like a very busy man of business doing business at his place of business in the early business morning—mimicking more or less everything I hated in the world—I strolled through the doors with the fast-but-not-hasty gait of a man who is Important and Knows It.

I glided right past the security desk. The fat guard didn't even glance up from the game on his iPad.

I glided to the nearest staircase. I've got a policy about elevators, which is to take them only if I'm going more than ten floors. I wasn't. At least, not initially.

I needed to find a directory, but pausing for the one in the lobby might have given the game away. So I paused as soon as I found the second floor, which had directory just in front of the elevator bank.

ADI Holdings was listed as 100. Tenth floor.

I hit the elevator button.

Chapter 8

Once on the floor, I used the front-facing camera on my phone to check my beard, hair, tie, suit. I buttoned the middle button of the jacket and opened the door to ADI Holdings.

Small office. Big view. One desk front left, and large chair, small fine-boned woman behind it. She had short, dark blonde hair that was swept back away from her temples, a little bristly in the back and sides. It was a good look against her tanned skin. She wore a gray business suit over a simple black shirt, gold earrings, a small stud in her nose.

I approached the desk, putting on Assured Smile #3.

"Hi there." I held out the card I'd slipped into my palm. "I'm here to talk to Mr. Kennelly."

She did not reach for the card, but did give me a smile I'd best describe as forced. It occurred to me that I'd be very interested in what a non-forced smile looked like on her. "Mr. Kennelly has no appointments today." Her hands moved on her desk in a way I didn't quite register as important.

"Well," I said, "I don't have an appointment, but it is very important that I speak to him. It's about his son."

Something passed across her features when I said that. Regret, I thought, her mouth turning down. Her eyes widened a tad. They were large, brown, soft. I liked looking at them.

But she still didn't take the card.

"Has something happened to Gabriel?"

"I don't know, but I'm trying to find out. That's why I'm here."

Her frown deepened. She grabbed a card and a pen and scribbled on it quickly, handed it over.

"Look, I just want to talk to Mr. Kennelly if it's at all possible. His son is…"

"I'm sorry," she mouthed as I took the card. I glanced down at it and saw a name—Gen, and a phone number with a 302 area code on it—when I heard the office door open.

I sighed. I slipped the card into my pocket and turned to face them.

Two men. Beefy, short haircuts, ill-fitting suits that didn't do anything to hide the muscles in their arms and shoulders. Ties that they wore like heavy collars. Their jackets were not buttoned, and they definitely wore weapons on their belts. I had no intention of finding out just what they carried. Wires snaked up into earpieces in their left ears.

I put hands up at chest level, palms out. "Gentlemen," I said. "That's a pretty impressive response time. I was just having a conversation with Gen here."

"You were just leaving," one of them said with a humorless tough-guy tone.

I'll admit that part of me wanted to find out then and there just how tough these guys were. Could be they were both holster-sniffers; the kind of losers who had gym muscles but never had the sand to enlist and were too stupid to get into any real police force, but wanted everyone to look at them as though they had authority.

Could also be they were both fifty-dollar an hour off-duty cops and retired Army Rangers. I figured that getting my ass handed to me in front of Gen was probably a bigger loss than I was prepared to take today.

The non-verbal one reached out and grabbed me by the cuff. I snatched my arm away.

"I'm leaving, boys. No need to get handsy."

He reached out for me again, and once more, I slipped his grip. I'd only got the one suit, after all.

"I said there's no need to get handsy. I'm goin'."

The non-talker—one blue eye, one brown—glanced at the other guy, who shrugged.

"We'll walk you to the door," the talker said.

"It's right there. I think I can find it." Behind me, I heard Gen snicker a little.

"The front door," he grunted. "No more talking."

"Fine, fine." I turned and gave Gen a little wave. Her smile turned a bit more genuine.

They went out the door ahead of me—there were probably not too many office doors that could've handled the two of them abreast, much less all three of us.

As I pulled the door closed behind us, I carefully dropped the card I'd been trying to hand the receptionist onto the beige carpet. The two security guards were too busy adjusting their cuffs and looking tough to notice.

They walked me to the elevator. "You know, I've got a rule," I said, "how I don't take the elevator if I'm going less than ten flights. And these are all downhill, so what's the harm…"

The non-talker twitched his wrist, and his hand was suddenly filled with a couple of feet worth of steel baton. "Fine, fine. We'll take the elevator. Gonna be close quarters, though. We're all big guys."

The button pinged with the arrival of the car. One held open the door and the other ushered me in. I put my back against the wall.

They crowded in ahead of me.

"You guys are in shape. Where do you work out?"

Silence.

"I go to Waterfront Fitness, bit off of Pulaski down in Cecil County? Small, but it's kind of old school, you know. Maybe you've got a corporate gym. Is there one on site here? That'd be a nice perk. Thinking well of their employees."

More silence. I don't deal well with silence when I'm anxious. I wouldn't have categorized it as a menacing silence, though. Not yet.

"So do you work for ADI Holdings, or the building, or a contractor?"

The talker turned around to glare at me. "You trying to be clever?"

I smiled. "Just making conversation."

He turned away, and for the last few seconds of the ride, I only had the off-kilter shoulders of their suit jackets to look at. Finally, we reached the ground floor. One got out, the other held the door. I made straight for the exit, but the tap of the knob on the end of the baton on my shoulder stopped me. He gestured toward the security desk with the baton, where the talker was already jawing at the fat desk guy. He was busy pulling out a phone, a handful of paper, and a clipboard.

Goddammit. I do not have the time to stand here and get a trespass order.

"I get what you're doing, gents. Just don't have the time to sit around and initial anything. I'll be on my way."

I turned. The baton tapped me on the shoulder again, harder this time. I spun around, grabbed the end of it.

"I've only got this one suit. It ain't much, but it's mine. You ruin it with that thing, and I'm gonna kick seventy dollars' worth of your ass."

"You paid seventy bucks for that? Got ripped off." The nontalker had a flat midwestern accent now that he finally spoke. I'd been privately hoping for Eastern European.

"Maybe I did, but it's all Penney's had in my size. I bet if I head to the mall now I could catch the end-of-season sales on the summer-weight stuff, though, so off I go."

I took half a step back. He snapped the baton against my arm, hard. It was supposed to be an arm-deadener, hit a nerve. But I'd seen it coming and curled my arm up, tensed the muscle. It smarted, but not anything more. I grabbed the end of the baton and wrenched it out of his hand; he was too surprised that his little move hadn't worked to hold on to it. I tossed it lightly a few steps away.

"Fetch," I said, then turned for the door.

The talker took a few steps after me. "You're trespassed here. We've got your face on the security camera and we'll have your license plate soon. Whatever you're doing, leave Mr. Kennelly and ADI out of it."

"If Mr. Kennelly is interested in where his son is, I expect I'll hear from him," I said. I gave the automatic door an extra push and headed out into the too-bright September morning.

Well, I thought. *That could've gone better.*

Chapter 9

By the time I was in the car and back on the road—with a triple espresso over ice, courtesy of a downtown coffee shop—I reflected on my failures. They were, as usual, legion. But I still had the receptionist's card, and she, hopefully, had mine. There was a contact to follow up on. And all in all it seemed likely that Tom Kennelly was so insulated from whatever went on with his son that everyone assumed he wouldn't care the kid was missing. That kind of assumption wasn't always right.

Just because he was an asshole didn't mean he was a *malicious* asshole. He might just be your average rich, uninterested dad. If I had to track him down on a golf course in Pennsylvania somewhere, I would. But for now, I thought I might as well waste a little time and head to Farrington.

I made it down to Furnace Bay in good time and circled past the place a couple of times. Ideally I'd park a long ways away and walk around it a few times, but that might just arouse suspicion at a school.

I concluded that an early lunch was hardly a bad thing. Going forth into virtuous battle with a full stomach and so on. I parked in a municipal lot and wandered the streets. I found a little sidewalk restaurant advertising a duck breast salad as its lunch special and decided I'd be remiss if I didn't try it, but only after I'd done some figuring of the calories and macros on an app where I recorded everything I ate and every workout.

While I ate, I filed a quick report that my attempt at contact this morning had been a failure, but that further contacts might come of it. I entered Gen into the case file as "principal-father/associate" and was about to enter the number she'd given me, but stopped short. That felt like an avenue that needed exploring in a personal way before I gave the info she'd given me to the firm.

No, not because I had designs. Not only. She had very nice eyes. I just had no way of knowing what that number was. For all I knew, she might've scribbled down the dad's number.

The salad was excellent, though I had them hold the cherry-ginger dressing. The server dropped off a small basket of bread, still warm. I stared it down every time I put greenery in my mouth, but emerged victorious.

With lunch over, I still had some time. Mulling over that phone number, I looked at the card again. Impulsively, I dialed it.

Three quick rings, then a voicemail.

"You've reached Gen. Please leave a mess—"

I hung up before the voicemail could really pick up. Definitely her number. Good to know.

There was nothing else but to walk around a bit, killing time. I'd have preferred to sit in the car and read but I hadn't thought to bring a book, and I was on company time anyway. Ultimately, I distracted myself with shops selling bric-a-brac and tchotchkes they branded as antiques until I could plausibly pull up to the school.

Furnace Bay had grown up around the school and there was a school-affiliated store carrying pennants, sweaters, and prints of the primary buildings, the football stadium, the boathouse, and the tennis courts. One could get a mug, a pen, a jacket, a Christmas tree ornament, a folder, a binder, a laptop skin, or a phone case with the Farrington logo on it.

There were also stores catering to the income bracket the parents likely belong to. Lots of thin sweaters, athleisure that didn't look ready for a workout, a yacht supply store, coffee shops. There was a marina down in the bay—it was being charitable to truly call it a bay—below the school and the town's main streets.

I was pretty sure if I'd ever tried to pull the *Belle* into a slip there, a credit rating alarm would go off and they'd turn a water cannon on me.

Farrington was an impressive edifice, no doubt. Cornices and towers and cupolas, ivy climbing the walls, beautifully manicured athletic fields. Students were streaming out onto those as I drove up the winding school path. A football team in practice whites and blue helmets with a decal of a rifle-toting colonial on the side. Soccer teams, field hockey, and the poorest bastards of all, the cross-country runners. Each and every one of them, from the thinnest eighth grader who glided an inch above the ground, to the slightly heavier kid determined to use the season to effect a change in himself, was secretly miserable. I knew it. They knew it. The world knew it. Their smiles and youthful, triumphant shouting couldn't hide the truth from me.

I'm a detective, dammit.

Chapter 10

I found the guest parking easily enough, did a quick beard, hair, and teeth check in the mirror. Popped a couple of mints, exited the car, remembered to button my suit jacket on the way up to the entrance. I pulled out my wallet so that my license was visible.

There was a call box in a prominent position by the front door. I pressed it, holding my face in front of what I presumed to be a camera lens, along with my license.

The box buzzed to life. "Who is it?"

"Jack Dixon," I said. "Investigator with Dent-Clark. Here for a two-thirty appointment."

The box buzzed and I heard the door unlock. I pushed my way in.

I have never liked school buildings, and I could tell right away that Farrington was not going to do anything to change that. Carpeted in what I could only describe as Institutional Beige, with fake gas-lamps on the walls. Paintings of founders and prominent alumni donors glowered at me from the walls. I glowered back before following the sign that directed me to the receptionist.

Time to finally come face to face with Amy Riordan.

I saw the desk with her nameplate on it, and my first thought, quite honestly, was that she'd called in sick and had a replacement in. The woman behind the desk was younger than me — between my age and Brock's I'd guess—with red hair carefully pinned back in a bun. She wore a blue dress I'd hesitate to call prim given the way it fit, though there was nothing suggestive or unprofessional about the cut. It was simply the way she wore it. Subtle makeup, in tones working off the dress. Dark frame eye glasses.

"Ms. Riordan?" I managed, despite being staggered by the weight of my own misapprehension.

"Yes." She smiled. I fought the urge to rush outside and rip some flowers out of the school's carefully tended plots along the walk way. "Mr. Dixon?"

"The same." I came forward with my wallet open to show my ID and license.

"You're not…carrying a weapon by any chance?"

Only my charm. Only my smile.

"No, miss. Wouldn't dream of it."

She turned around a tablet and held out a stylus. Her nails were painted a shade to match the dress. I kept noticing these things. There was a great deal about Amy Riordan to notice. She had green eyes. The forearms that extended from the sleeves of her dress were toned. The jewelry she wore all matched or complimented the color of her dress.

I took the stylus and clicked to indicate that I was fulfilling the appointment, then squiggled a signature where the screen indicated. She turned the tablet back to her, took the stylus, and indicated a seat just across from her desk.

I sat. I felt far too large for the seat, as it was likely designed with mischievous children in mind. I thought about dragging a second one over for support, but then I felt Ms. Riordan's eyes on me and decided that stoic suffering was the only course.

"Sorry I asked about a weapon, I just…you hear detective, you think…" She shrugged. It was one of the most arresting shrugs I'd ever seen.

"It's all right, Ms. Riordan. Sometimes we do have to carry them, but I don't like to unless I really feel like I must. Nine out of ten days, there's just no reason."

She smiled a little more warmly. "Amy is fine, Mr. Dixon."

"Going to insist on Jack then."

Stop flirting and ask her some investigative questions. Detect something.

Looked like she was about to beat me to the punch. "So, you're looking for Gabe?"

I nodded. "His mom retained me yesterday. Did this come out of nowhere?"

She sighed. "He wasn't a happy kid, not really. Not my place to say, I guess."

"How so?"

She shrugged again. I focused.

"I've only been here since last year. As an employee, I mean. I'm a Farrington alumna, from a few years ago, and working on my master's in secondary ed, and my state certification. The school helps pay for it," she said, unburdening herself in the way someone who felt compelled to explain why their situation didn't match their ambition would do, given the space. "Anyway, I knew Gabe as a younger student, a bit. He never seemed to live up to all of his potential. And this year, it just got worse," she said, lowering her voice and looking to the door to her left, my right.

I was working hard to remember the important parts of what she was saying. I wanted to get my notebook out of my jacket pocket and start scribbling it down, but that might make her stop talking.

People will keep talking all day provided they believe you're listening *and* not recording what they say.

"He wasn't going to go out for cross-country, or so they said."

"Well, I can hardly blame the kid for not wanting to run. Might as well go home and hit yourself in the shins for an hour, right?"

She did chuckle at that. "Mr. Dixon, I doubt you have that much trouble with a little exercise."

My heart swelled. So might have my chest and my arms, a little less involuntarily than the heart.

"Anyway, there were colleges looking at Gabe for cross-country and track. Big universities. West Virginia, UVA, Temple, to name a few."

A kid suddenly turning sullen at age eighteen wasn't unheard of.

Neither was it unheard of for that kind of shift to be the byproduct of a pharmaceutical habit.

"He have friends?"

Amy nodded, and looked about to say more when the office door next to us swung open.

Dr. Elijah Marks stood there. I'm reasonably sure I would've known who he was even if his name hadn't been on the door or his picture not on the website. He was in three-piece summer-weight tweed, a light green, with a brilliantly-shined silver watch chain gleaming against the vest. Silver spectacles rode low on his nose, and his beard was graying and cropped close against his dark mahogany skin.

I stood up, as did Amy. "Mr. Dixon from the Clark-Dent agency."

I took half a step forward and extended my hand. He took it. Strong grip, for an academic. He turned and waved me into his office. I followed, but not without turning around and giving Amy the most charming smile I could muster, a little twist of the mouth upward at the left corner. A faint wave.

She smiled back, stifled a giggle, and waved.

This was looking like a potentially fruitful visit no matter what I found.

Chapter II

The walls of Dr. Marks' office were surrounded by glass-fronted bookcases, each one full. There was a long conference table at the far end, where he waved me to a seat. A few scattered folders lay on the table.

He picked one up, settling into a chair just a few feet away from me.

"Here looking for Gabriel Kennelly, hrm?"

"Yes, sir."

He eyed me over the folder and the curve of his glasses. "Why are you looking for Gabriel Kennelly?"

"His mother hired me, sir."

He closed the folder and set it down, tapping one thick finger on it. "It is a great shame when we lose a student that way, dropping out. Still can't believe it's even *legal*. What'll you do if you find him?"

"When I find him, I'll tell his mother where he is. I'll try to find out what he wants. And if he's in some kind of trouble, I'll do what I can to help him out of it."

"When?"

I nodded. "Doesn't help to be negative, sir."

"All these *sirs*. Military man?"

"Navy, sir."

"Hrm." He smiled faintly. "Nobody's perfect, but some are better than others." His eyes flitted to the top shelf of a bookcase behind his desk, and I saw it: a shadowbox with a black background, red sergeant's stripes, and several rows worth of ribbons and medals I couldn't identify from this far away. And there, on his desk in a penholder, was a small USMC flag.

I smiled back. "I don't suppose there's any chance Gabriel went and enlisted, is there?"

"Local recruitment offices were the first calls I made, after his parents," Dr. Marks said. "Pays to have a relationship with them, managing this many young people. Some will find their path taking them there. But none of them had seen Gabriel, or a boy matching his description."

I nodded. I had no reason to believe Dr. Marks hadn't done that, but I was still going to have to check into it myself. Trust, but verify.

"Who do you want to talk to?"

"Well, I was told my appointment would be with the Dean of Student Life, but I wasn't told who that was."

"Mr. Gunter," Dr. Marks said. "But who do you *want* to talk to?"

"If Gabriel had a roommate, him. A romantic interest, them. Close friends or teammates. A teacher he had a special relationship with. A counselor if Gabriel ever visited. Anyone you think might help."

Dr. Marks fixed me with a hard stare. "I count myself a good judge of people, Mr. Dixon. As far as I can tell, you're here to help. But if I find you causing the slightest disturbance to my staff or especially my students, I will drag you out of here. By your ear if I have to. Is that clear?"

"As a bell, sir."

He nodded. "Good. Mr. Gunter's office is just down the corridor. Turn right out of here, on your left. He's…energetic," Dr. Marks said, in a way I could tell didn't quite signify disapproval. But he was trying to warn me. "Tell him I've asked him to cooperate with you. But you do understand that the school won't reveal anything confidential."

I lifted my hands, palms out. "Of course. Wouldn't ask it."

Oh, I would. And Mr. Gunter might not be too terribly aware of what was or wasn't, strictly speaking, in a legal sense, confidential.

Dr. Marks stood, and I gathered that our interview was at an end. He extended his hand. I took it. His grip was still as strong as it had been a few minutes ago. I was less surprised, though, given the stripes in the shadowbox on the wall.

Chapter 12

I exited Dr. Marks' office to the radiant smile of Amy Riordan. A lesser man might've been halted in his tracks. But she also had a phone squeezed between ear and shoulder, and was nodding along with the words of the person on the other end.

Keen investigator's insight told me it *wasn't* the time to stop and flirt. I soldiered on, and found Mr. Gunter's office with little trouble. I passed a few students in the halls. Khakis, blue or white blazers, plaid ties, the occasional plaid skirt. Plastic smiles that papered over a kid's natural curiosity. I knew that kids had a keen sense for when something had intruded, was missing, or was different. Kids could be a wonderful source of information for the resourceful investigator.

At the same time, I recognized that my position in the school was a bit precarious, and asking questions of a minor without some precautions taken was both a rocky and a shady road lined with thirsty litigators and vengeful judges.

Not to mention the fact that I didn't want to be the kind of detective who braced a *child*.

So I just avoided their eyes and found myself tapping on Mr. Gunter's door, which was cracked enough to swing open as soon as I knuckled it. A far too cheerful voice invited me in.

Posters on the walls, a mountain with an Epictetus quote about what you would be. Another mountain, with the Aristotle quote about excellence being a habit. What looked like a custom-printed banner with, of all damned things, a Soren Kierkegaard quote, behind his desk.

"The challenge must be made difficult, for only the difficult inspires the noble-hearted."

He must've seen me looking at it, because Mr. Gunter read it aloud. I looked at him, below the banner, standing behind a desk that was probably not quite as large as Dr. Marks', but in half the office, it looked twice the size. The desk had a huge monitor on it, a number of pictures, and a tripled deck of plastic shelves for inbox, outbox, and, I guess, wildcard. Mr. Gunter himself looked to be perhaps thirty and just full of energy. He wore a pink dress shirt tucked into blue dockers, no tie, pale gold cufflinks. His skin glowed with the ruddy tan of the habitually healthy. He was skinny, had close-cropped blond hair, and blue eyes.

He extended his hand, his smile a gleam of brilliant pearl. I hated him a little already. His grip was not as strong as that of his boss.

"Soren Kierkegaard," he finished, jutting his chin—dimpled like Viggo Mortensen's—toward the poster. "A Danish philosopher and theologian."

I bit back the urge to unburden everything I knew about Kierkegaard, which was mostly relegated to a dog-eared copy of *Fear and Trembling* I had occasionally tried to puzzle my way through since I took a class on him my second year in college.

"You must be Jack Dixon," he said, waving toward a chair. It was a soft-backed wraparound kind. I did not fit in it comfortably, while he leaned back in a leather executive number.

"And you must be Mr. Gunter, Dean of Student Life."

"Matt," he said, with the same smile. I felt like he was out to sell me a car I didn't want.

"Well, Matt. Hopefully, Dr. Marks has filled you in on what I'm here for."

"He mentioned it," he said, leaning forward, indicating interest. "But let's start fresh."

"Gabriel Kennelly."

"Yes," Matt said. He leaned further forward and planted his elbows on the edge of his desk. Still smiling. Felt like I was being sold on the undercoat.

"He dropped out. Seems to have disappeared. His mother has retained me to find him."

"Isn't that typically a police matter?"

"It would be if he were a minor," I said, trying not to grind my teeth. "But as you probably know…"

"Gabe did turn eighteen just a few days ago," he said, leaning back once more. He lifted his left leg and let the ankle rest on his right knee. Casual. Trying to push a detailing package.

"Yes," I confirmed. "So it's not really a police matter, or it wouldn't be for a while. That's where I come in."

"You've got experience in these kinds of things, then?"

"I'm an investigator."

He simply smiled at me, blandly.

"I've found people who didn't want to be found before, yes."

"And what can I do for you?"

"Give me a list of Gabriel's closest friends, let me talk to his roommate, and so on."

"Well, I can't just turn you loose on the school, Mr. Dixon."

"I'm well aware of that. Any questioning I do of any of your students should be done with a member of the faculty—preferably administration—present. Of course. I'd also like to talk to your counselor, if I could."

"Well, we have three counselors on staff."

"Any of them that have had contact with Gabriel, then."

"Right. So perhaps you could fill me in on — "

I am a *patient* man. It is among my best qualities. Perhaps my *only* claim to virtue. Patience is a baseline requirement to be any kind of investigator. But there's patient, and there's wasting time.

"Look, Matt. Dr. Marks told me you were to cooperate with me. I need to start speaking to some people with direct knowledge of Gabriel's habits and state of mind and I need to do it soon. If I have to recount the status and nature of my investigation to everyone I speak with, I will never find him."

"Understood," Matt said, rapping his bronzed knuckles on the surface of his desk. "Understood. A man of action. Let me get on the phone and you can start with a counselor, and I'll have a list of students, and we'll set you up with a meeting space."

He picked up his phone, quickly dialing it after referencing a faculty phone chart. I withdrew from his desk to give him some space, glancing at a rack of pamphlets on the wall. Leadership courses, scholarship programs, summer camps the school offered for year-round boarders and the like. I pretended to be engrossed while eavesdropping like hell.

"Hey, Cindy. Who had Kennelly, Gabriel?" A pause. "Thalheim? Is he free? Okay, someone he needs to talk to. Yes. About Gabriel." A few noncommittal noises. I read a pamphlet about the availability of polo teams in the surrounding area. I felt sorry for the horses.

The phone slammed down and I turned back to Matt.

"Dr. Thalheim will see you. Counseling suite is on the third floor, old wing. Elevator is…"

I closed the pamphlet, stuck it back in the wrong space, and exited, saying, "I'll find the stairs."

Chapter 13

By the time I found the counseling suite I could feel sweat gathering on my lower back, my suit was annoying me, and I felt I wasn't making one damn bit of progress.

The counseling suite door was an impressive dark wood, and it led to a central office with three other office doors within. Behind the desk was the woman I presumed to be Cindy—the desk plate said "Mrs. Ringsmith."

The woman stationed behind was a great deal more like what I'd expected from Amy Riordan. My smile seemed to bounce off of her matronly armor.

"I'm here to see Dr. Thalheim."

She pointed to the door to her left. I made directly for it.

"He may be a minute," she began in a voice that probably made most of the high school kids stop in their tracks. Luckily that voice hasn't worked on me for at least a couple of years now. I knocked on the door and let myself in.

This office exuded the kind of old money I'd expected out of the school. Green leather-backed chairs with brass accents. A desk so large it looked like it couldn't possibly be removed from the room without taking down a wall. Dark blue carpeting, pictures of sailboats and aerial photos of the school throughout the years on the wall.

Behind the desk was a man several years older than me, dark blond hair going a stately gray at the temples. His skin had a healthy glow. I started wondering if there was a tanning suite somewhere in this gigantic pile of a school.

He wore a bespoke light tan suit that put my off-the-rack gray to shame, a blue shirt, cufflinks, pink and blue striped tie, matching pocket square. His face was square, cheeks a little round. A bit of a belly strained the braces he wore under his jacket. Everybody at this school dressed better than I did.

"Mr. Dixon, I take it. He extended his hand. I nodded and took it. His hand wasn't limp, but it was clammy. I fought the urge to wipe my hand on my pants when I sat on the green leather and wood chair across the desk that he gestured to with his free hand. A watch the size of a banquet salad plate was strapped to his wrist. The surface was a rich blue color and there were a few subdials. It positively reeked of money.

He noticed me studying it and pulled the cuff of his shirt over top the watch.

"Nice watch," I muttered.

"It ought to be," he replied. There was an awkward pause and he went on. "So, here to talk about Gabriel Kennelly."

"Yes."

His desk was clear except for a green blotter, a couple of framed photos I couldn't see, and a penholder with two gold pens in it. I spared a moment to wonder if they were gold, plated, or just colored that way.

Clearly it was up to me to talk some more.

"Did you interact with Gabriel?"

"We divide the students up alphabetically, so I was responsible for any guidance services Gabriel would need. H through O," he said, grinning. His teeth were bright against his skin.

I did not like Dr. Thalheim. I wasn't sure why. Yet. But I was pretty sure he'd supply a reason.

"Well, what can you tell me about those interactions? Did you speak to him often?"

"We have at least yearly check-ins with every student. I don't have extensive notes of those meetings with Gabriel. He had his troubles, of course. Inattentive father. Pretty common around here, unfortunately."

"Was he making plans for the future? College? Military? Career?"

"Well, several schools were interested in Gabriel's career as a long-distance runner."

"Right. Was he excited about this?"

"Gabriel was a close-lipped sort of boy. You know, these days children don't like to show themselves excited about anything. I believe with time he would've seen the wisdom of taking one of these scholarships."

"In this day and age, with the costs of school, you'd figure a kid would get excited about the possibility of athletic scholarships."

"I don't think the Kennellys live in the same world as working men like you and me, Mr. Dixon. I doubt the impending costs of college bothered him very much. I am certain they didn't bother his father."

"Is there anything," I said, "that would lead you to believe that Gabriel would drop out? Any hint of where he might go?"

"If I had to guess, I'd say it's a ploy to get his father's attention. Setting state records in distance running wasn't doing the trick, so," he shrugged, "maybe he decided to run a little farther."

For a school guidance counselor, I thought Dr. Thalheim had a pretty cavalier attitude about a student disappearing.

"He have a significant other?"

"I try not to pay too much attention to a student's social life unless it is somehow impeding their success or health."

"You could just say you don't know, doc."

My instinctive dislike of the man was starting to harden. It was going to start showing any minute now.

"Well, then I don't know, Mr. Dixon" Dr. Thalheim put a lot of emphasis on the *mister*. I was being put in my place.

"I don't suppose you can tell me if Gabriel had any history of diagnoses of mental illness or emotional disturbance." I was starting to feel like the visit to the school had been a waste of time. But there were still leads to be run to ground here, if I could just get a glance at one.

"I'm afraid that we are verging on privileged information, Mr. Dixon." Dr. Thalheim smiled and I got another glimpse at that watch. I'm not someone who takes notice of watches, generally. But there was something about this one, the gaudiness of it, the gleam of the metal case.

"I see. Is it possible that I could view any records with permission from his mother?"

"I'm afraid Gabriel is no longer a minor."

I was being evaded. I couldn't see why this guy had any reason to do that. Even if he truly didn't care about the kids he was responsible for, he likely cared about the reputation of the school, and a kid dropping out and disappearing wouldn't do it any good.

I hoped that by this point Matt would have some students lined up for me to talk to. So I decided to cut my losses with Dr. Thalheim. I slipped a card out of the case in my pocket, scribbled my own number on the back, and slid it across his fortress of a desk.

"Doc, if you think of anything, I could really use a lead." Not like me to bare my soul like that, but perhaps it would move his clinical heart.

I left his office. As I closed the door behind me, I thought I heard the telltale click of a phone leaving its cradle.

Chapter 14

The next hour was spent in a student lounge, a room decorated as blandly as possible, with a couple rows of desks with study carrel and a pair of round tables in the middle. A teacher of impressive title and ancient provenance set up at a desk in the corner and promptly fell asleep and I decided he could be safely ignored. They set me up at a round table and brought in a succession of kids, one at a time. Track teammates. Junior year roommate. Kids who shared a schedule.

I got used to the barrage of questions they had for me so that by the time I got to the fourth, I could lead off.

"Yes, I'm really a private investigator. Yes, I used to be a cop. No, I'm not wearing a gun. No, I don't usually carry one. No, it's not anything like in the movies."

That about covered it so that I could get down to questioning them.

The picture that emerged of Gabriel was a little muddled. Cross-country and track teammates remembered him as a gifted runner. Unusually good, unusually smooth, never got rattled, but never seemed to care too much. Didn't always practice hard, because it seemed like he didn't need to.

His roommate said he was quiet, neat, didn't hang around the dormitory much.

They were teenagers, so many were a little sullen and a little distrustful. They had their reasons.

One of them near the end made more of an impression than the others. Elizabeth. There were two by that name on the list, and I wasn't sure which one I was talking to. She walked in as if it were entirely a waste of her time and sat facing me, with her eyes pointedly fixed on the wall behind me. She wore the school polo shirt with khakis. She carried a messenger bag, the strap and body of which were decorated with a profusion of enamel pins, most of which I was too old to understand. One, though, was the Rebel Alliance, red-on-black. She had blonde hair, pulled back into a plain ponytail.

"Elizabeth" I said. "I didn't catch your last name."

"I didn't say it."

"Could I have it, please?"

"Bathory de Ecsed."

I set my pen atop my notebook and stared at her.

She stared right back, eyes wide and bland and blameless.

"You are not a sixteenth century Hungarian countess."

She shrugged. "It was worth a shot. Mortimer-Hanes."

I could *smell* the money off of the hyphen in that last name alone.

"Thanks. You were friends with Gabe?"

"Gabriel. He didn't like being called Gabe."

"Sorry," I said. *That might be the first piece of useful information I've gotten today.* "Anything else you could tell me about him?"

"He was on cross-country and track."

"I know that," I said, sensing that Elizabeth might respond well to a little leveling-with. "I know he ran. I know he didn't seem to like it all that much. I know he was quiet and his roommate didn't really know him."

"He hates running."

I paused in the hopes she would go on. She didn't, so I said, "He hates running?"

She nodded vigorously, but didn't add anything.

"If he hated it, why did everyone who talked to me talk about it?"

"Probably because no one asked him what he actually thought. Most people are just waiting for their chance to talk."

Mary and all the Saints save me from a teenager performing cynicism.

"That's probably true. But if there's anything you can tell me that'll help me find Gabriel, I promise you, I'm listening."

She looked me dead in the eye then. "I don't know where he went, or really, why. I hope he'll come back. I think he will."

"He have a girlfriend or boyfriend he might've run off to see?"

"Way to not be hetero-normative about it," Elizabeth said. "But no, I don't think he was dating anybody."

"Something to do with his parents?"

"Isn't anything a teenager does about their parents?"

On the one hand, I kind of liked this kid. On the other, I had limited time and felt like I was starting to waste it.

"Look, Elizabeth."

"Liza."

"Liza, is there anything at all you can think of, no matter how inconsequential it seemed at the time, that might have indicated where Gabriel went?"

She shook her head. "I've texted him, snapped him, sent him email…nothing."

I took out another card, wrote my personal cell on it. "Listen. If you hear anything at all from him, please, *please* call me."

"Text," she said, though she did take the card and slide it into a pocket.

"Text is fine, too. If you hear anything, think of anything, let me know."

"Why do you care? Is it just a paycheck?"

I decided to try a little brute force honesty.

"Truth be told, Liza, I get paid via billable hours. Whether I find Gabriel or not doesn't really affect that."

"That's stupid."

"Lot of things are. But I want to find your friend."

"Why? Some kind of code of masculinity thing? You said you'd do it, you took the job, so you have to do it?"

"That's pretty much it, actually," I said. My voice sounded lame to my ears. Too quiet, without the confidence I'd been working to project since I walked in. I'm sure I deflated a little.

"Kind of sad to define yourself based on a job."

"Pick the things that matter and live 'em out, Liza. That's the sum total of the wisdom I've got. So I'm gonna do whatever I can to find Gabriel."

"If you say 'I promise.'" She almost sneered.

My phone buzzed in my pocket. I glanced at it. A Wilmington area code. I wasn't entirely sure, but it might have been the number Gen had written on the business card she'd given me.

"Look, Liza. I've got to take this, and I've probably accomplished all I can here today. If you think of anything…"

"Text or fax or send you a courier with a sealed bag or a falcon with a tube tied to its leg, right." She stood up and stomped out of the room, the pins on her bag jingling lightly.

I answered the phone.

"Jack Dixon," I said.

"Mr. Dixon? It's Gen, from the ADI office."

"Hi, Gen. You have some useful information for me or is this a social call?"

A chuckle, but a worried one, I thought. "I would like to talk to you about…that matter. Could you meet me?"

"I'm a little ways outside Wilmington, but sure."

"Well, we could meet halfway."

Chapter 15

Soon I was speeding back north into Delaware. But not before I'd stopped in the main office on my way out, to drop another card with my number on Amy Riordan's desk.

She had smiled. Winsomely. I had smiled. Winningly. Small talk was exchanged. Dimples formed on her cheeks.

I have a strict policy of not trying too hard to pick up anyone I encounter while actively engaged in an investigation. But for Ms. Riordan I think I was willing to make an exception.

That being said, I thought I should try and find Gabriel Kennelly as soon as I could, just to clear my conscience on the matter.

Gen had asked to meet in a county park in Glasgow, right off of Route 40. I hadn't gotten out of the school till after four—lots of kids to talk to, and the only one who'd mattered at all had been holding back. So had Dr. Thalheim, for that matter. Lots to think about as I meandered through rush hour traffic.

How did people *do* this every day?

Eventually I found the park and guided my car into a space. I dug out a key and opened the lockbox, pondering the Taser.

"Pretty sure I can take Gen, if it comes to it."

I slipped a few things into my pockets, but didn't clip the weapon to my belt, and got out of the car. I discarded the tie and left the pocket square for that casual look.

She was sitting on a bench within sight of the parking lot, her back to me. I knew it was her, though. Same suit, same excellent fit, same intriguingly sleek haircut. She looked nervous, twitchy, barely at rest. She kept looking at anyone that passed her, and finally back over her shoulder at the parking lot.

I was never much for sneaking, and the Navy didn't really teach me camouflage. Bigger than most of the folks around me in most rooms, a beard, ill-fitting suit; I wasn't anything approaching incognito. She spotted me, stood quickly, and waved.

She was still wearing her work clothes but had traded out whatever kind of shoes she'd been wearing for vibrant orange running shoes. They stood out against the gray and black she wore, and looked like serious runner's gear. They were well worn, too.

No choice now but to approach. She was clearly nervous, practically buzzing with unspent energy. But she did try a smile. Despite her nerves, it was a good look.

Given how obviously anxious she was, I stayed several feet away—well out of arm's length. "Everything alright?"

She nodded vigorously. "Just…can we take a walk? There's some benches along the trails. I'd rather be in private."

I did not like what was happening. Something in my gut. Could be I just didn't like seeing Gen quite so nervous, fearful I might be the cause. Could've been something else. She glanced from side to side as we spoke.

"Sure," I said. I decided to cast about for some small talk, in the hopes of calming her down a bit. "You come running here? Those shoes don't look like they're for show."

She nodded. "Couple of times a week, longer distance. Mix it up with light weights and high-impact at the gym. You work out?"

"Every day I can manage it."

"Like to run?"

"About as much as I like dentists and kale," I said.

She laughed a little. By then we'd walked into the tree line. "Bench up here," she said, around a curve of the trail. I could see it in the late autumn shadows.

And I could see two shadows looming near it that *weren't* trees, joggers, or dog-walkers.

"Gen." I turned to look at her. She was backing away, frightened.

"I'm sorry," she whispered, before she turned and took off.

Even with no warm-up, no stretching, and in office-wear, the lady could move. I'll give her that.

I turned toward my suited pals from ADI holdings, who were advancing. I took a couple of steps forward. No point in showing fear, even if I was pretty sure I was about to get my ass kicked.

I slipped my hands into my pockets while the two guys fanned out in front of me. The earpieces were gone. I did a quick weapons check. Neither had a gun out, nor the bulge of one on their belt. But the fellow with the differently colored eyes and the flat midwestern accent still had his baton. Collapsed, but wrapped up in his fist. Either way it could do some damage. That made him my priority.

"You're gonna be fetchin' your fuckin' teeth," he drawled at me.

"Come get 'em, Fargo," I sneered while I slipped my hands out of my pockets. I wished I wasn't wearing dress shoes as I spread my feet and felt for purchase on the asphalt of the walking path. I wanted to shrug my coat off but I couldn't take the risk of getting my arms tangled.

A metallic snap as the baton came into his hand. He rushed forward. I raised my hand and unleashed a stream of law enforcement-grade pepper spray straight into his eyes.

I squatted and shuffled back a few steps to avoid the cloud. From his sudden gagging I thought some had probably gotten into his mouth.

"You son of a bitch," he gasped while his friend barreled straight past him and tried to throw a tackle on me.

I tried to turn with the momentum, throw out a leg, and toss him to the ground. But he wasn't having it and got his hands on me. We both stumbled until we were on the grass and my shoes went out from under me on a slick patch.

He came down with me, tried to headbutt me, but my backwards fall wasn't totally useless. I was able to bring a knee up into his ribcage a couple of times. He went for my chin, which I'd tucked into my chest, tensing the muscles of my neck. I tried to hip-heist and get my way back to my feet, but dress shoes on muddy grass weren't designed for that. If I still had any chops, it might not have mattered, but all I accomplished was to nearly get out of his grip and then hurl myself backwards. At least the landing hurt him, as he grunted hard when we hit. He started trying to get his hands at my tucked chin. I threw my weight to one side and pushed with as many limbs as I could get involved. He spun off of me and scrambled to his feet. I followed him and we stared warily at one another.

He tore off his jacket, so I did the same. He was wearing a hip holster that was mercifully empty.

"You gonna pepper-spray me like a little bitch?" he snarled.

"That depends, are you gonna send another guy with a steel baton after me?"

He came on. I tried a jab. He slipped it to his shoulder and then came the body blows. He got several good ones into my ribs. I got a couple into his, and lowered my head, hard, into the side of his. For a few moments, there was just the snap of sharp breaths, the thud of punches landing. I butted him again, opening a gash along the side of his head.

I'd like to suggest it was a deadly ballet of athletic grace. It was a lot of sweaty grunting, really, like most of these things were. I'd spent enough time on mats and in cages to know that. I tried to throw him over my hip again, and all I got for it was a chorus of suddenly protesting back muscles.

He slipped my clinch and tried to back away. All I really had was reach, so I went for it and snapped two jabs into his face. The first one wasn't square, but the second was, and I saw his eyes widen with it, the sudden shock of pain, the moment of ringing emptiness. Anybody who's really been hit knows what that feels like and learns to recognize it in the opponent.

I was ready to move in, pin him to the ground, and choke him out. I could've done it. I knew it. I felt it rising in me. He was just stunned enough. I was hurt, but I felt old wrestling instincts kicking in.

But I hesitated. His eyes cleared. The moment passed, and I readied myself to get even more of an ass-kicking than I already had.

Behind us I heard a shriek. He looked, still a little in stupor. I backed away and glanced.

A couple of middle-aged women in walking clothes, light weights in their hands, had come upon the scene. One hitter on the ground, loudly retching and trying to rub his eyes with handfuls of grass. Two more circling each other, shirts torn and grass stained, probably bleeding.

It must've been like stumbling onto a horror movie.

"Call 911," one of the ladies yelled, and they turned and made pretty good time down the path.

We looked warily at each other. "Ain't neither of us wants to be here when the cops show," I said. "And you ought to get your friend some medical attention."

"That was a bitch move."

"You like that word too much," I spat. I felt my lips swelling and my ribs creaking up. "Are we done here?"

"Here, yeah," he said. "Gonna get him fixed and come looking for you."

"Good," I said. "We wouldn't want little Fargos running around trying to hit everyone with sticks when they get agitated."

We warily circled to pick up our jackets. I backed away until I was down the path, then I broke into a jog and made it to the car.

On the way there, everything *really* started to hurt.

Chapter 16

had pulled out and driven to the nearest shopping center, where I parked in the thickest concentration of nondescript cars, before I heard the sirens. A single county car went by, followed by a state trooper. The response time was good, if not great, but my guess is the two women hadn't offered a great description of the combatants.

I tried a deep breath. I imagined I could hear my ribs cracking. My back screamed in protest. It was going to be an ugly couple of days. I could feel some bruises blooming along my chin, and my neck and back were no picnic. My suit and dress shirt were a ruin.

I sat back in the seat, wincing. In the meantime, I tried to organize my thoughts by entering them in the app. I entered all the new contacts, typing them meticulously from the notebook. I only entered a few with the tag "priority." Liza, Dr. Thalheim, Matt Gunter, Dr. Marks. I hovered over typing Amy Riordan in.

On the one hand, I definitely wanted a chance to speak to her again. On the other, putting her into a case file was, perhaps, crossing an ethical line. There was yet *another* ethical line in leaving her off, however, since she did know the principal, presumably the client, and may have valuable information.

"Goddammit," I breathed as I tapped her name in on my phone.

By the time I was done entering my list of contacted people, the sun had vanished and the sky had gone purple. I was sore, hungry, tired, probably nursing a broken rib, and I needed to get back to the office. I tapped out a text to Jason, asking him to stay put, since I was bringing the car in.

My phone quickly pinged.

Keep it. You'll need it tomorrow.

I wasn't entirely sure that I would, since I had no idea where to go or what to do about this case now. Perhaps sleep would illuminate some things. Sleep and food. Sleep and food and whiskey.

"The three pillars of a good evening," I muttered. I started the car up and maneuvered back out into traffic.

On the way I kept a half-hearted eye out for a tail, but I didn't think I'd see Fargo and his minder again quite so soon. I'd definitely done a number on him with the spray.

The extent to which the other, for whom I'd not yet found a snappy sobriquet, had kicked some or all of my ass was worrying. I hadn't been in the gym to practice, only to lift and run, for a couple of months. My punches were soft, my stances off, and my ground game an absolute shambles. I needed to fix that if I was going to keep catching cases like this.

That was a problem for tomorrow, though. Just after I crossed the border back into Maryland, I pulled briefly off of 40 and parked in front of a Capriotti's. I wanted to order an absurdly large turkey, stuffing, and cranberry sub. I stared at the front window of the shop. I could taste it.

I pulled away, drove back to the marina a defeated man, and lugged myself, my ruined jacket, and the Taser back to the *Belle*.

I set the Taser and my phone down on a table I had out on the deck, and went down into the main cabin to change. I threw the ruined suit jacket and pants on the floor. It felt good. Then I bent down and gathered them up, put them on the hanger, and wrapped the blue garment bag around them once again. I got on a t-shirt and some shorts. From my dopp kit in the head I took out a bottle of aspirin and spilled three into the palm of my hand.

Then to the galley. I considered making a cocktail. Then I took the bottle of rye, pulled the cork loose, and stumbled out onto the deck. I grabbed the last jar of peanut butter out of the fridge, and an apple from the basket on the table.

I opened the peanut butter, mixed it with a finger, and took a half spoonful. I tossed the aspirin in and sent a gulp of rye after them. Just to be sure they had all the assistance they needed, I sent another.

When I got halfway through dinner, and halfway through the third of the rye that had been in the bottle, I started trying to piece it all together.

"If the kid had fled to his dad, there's no reason to hide that. So why send a couple of pipe-hitters after me? If that was even the dad's decision. Might just be the standard corporate response to a nosy PI."

I spoke aloud, just me and the boat and the water. None of my neighbors in this particular marina lived in their boats.

I had a sudden paranoid impulse to fire up the engines and take the *Belle* out of the marina, into a channel, find a secluded cove to drop anchor and sleep. They had my name and employer, but it's not as though they had a fixed address.

I shoved that thought down while I chewed some more.

What exactly hadn't I liked about Dr. Thalheim?

"He treated me like an imposition," I said aloud. "Which I was."

But Gabriel's well-being shouldn't have been.

Dr. Thalheim was paid to care about the well-being of the children at Farrington. By the looks of it, well paid. The watch, the suit, even his smile. They all *glowed* with wealth. I didn't like it, but then, I had the prole's instinctive distrust of the slickly moneyed.

One day into my first investigation in weeks, and what did I have?

"Busted ribs, back spasms, a couple of burned contacts, and not a goddamned clue."

I stood and paced the deck for a few minutes. Then I turned on my radio and tuned in the Orioles, who were losing to Toronto again. But the comforting drone of it mixed with the lapping of the water against the hull settled me.

I finished my apple, took one more tablespoon of peanut butter than I typically ate. The Orioles threatened in the seventh, loading the bases. An infield pop fly and a groundball back to the pitcher settled that.

I finished the rye. It wasn't late, but I was done with the day. I turned everything off, set the alarm on my phone, and climbed into bed.

Chapter 17

I hadn't had a chance to change the song on the alarm. So Guy Clark was well onto the last verse of *L.A. Freeway* by the time it finally dragged me awake.

I was *made* of pain. Aspirin was not going to get the job done.

"Whiskey might," I said aloud, to the calls of the herons and ducks.

I don't drink in the mornings while on a job. Or, usually, at all. Was this a special day?

"No," I said. I gathered my will and forced myself to sit upright. I unplugged my tablet and typed up a quick email to Jason.

No good developments. Got my ass kicked a little. Not sure why. Will be in late.

He'd stew over that, but I needed to seek some treatment to get into working shape. So I texted Dani.

Gonna be at the club today?

It took a minute for that to switch from "Delivered" to "Read." Then she typed an answer.

Already here. You have twenty minutes before I leave.

I sighed, dressed in some of the loosest clothes I had—green sweatpants, an XXL t-shirt that read "HUZZAH" on the front and had been a gift from someone who wasn't real clear on sizing. Tying my Chucks had me swearing up a streak I hadn't unleashed since the last time some dumb kitchen trainee had ruined an entire oven's worth of chicken paillards.

And then, rather than walk, I swallowed my pride and drove over to Waterfront Fitness.

For just that moment I could see the appeal. I was in pain. It was hot. The car offered climate control, ease of use, rapid movement. All of these things came with a cost, though, and it was still one I wasn't all that ready to pay.

I pulled in just a few minutes later. It was a seductive machine, for all that it was a boxy piece of crap.

I stumbled in the door without even my usual gym bag, just my phone and my water bottle, and ran straight into Nick. He wore the same tight orange Under Armour staff shirt, and the same bright, helpful smile.

Until he got a look at my face.

"Jesus, Mr. Dixon. What happened?"

I shrugged. "Occupational hazard. You should see the other guy?"

"Why? What happened to *him*?"

"Might be blind," I said as I shrugged past him and made a sharp right, away from the weights and resistance machines and treadmills, down a corridor with separate classrooms. One held a pair of heavy bags on stands and the floor was heavily matted.

In it, a woman in tight athletic gear gave a mixture of commands and encouragement to two out of shape guys practicing basic takedowns on the mat. They sweated with the exertion of simply lunging forward to grab at the other's wobbly leg. Good for them. Bad for me.

The woman instructing them was about my height, and sculpted out of wood. She was the kind of person sweat-wicking athletic wear had been designed to fit. She had dark hair but kept it cut very short. There were tattoos along the sides of her skull: names. I couldn't quite read them.

She shouted a few words of encouragement, telling Josh to squat, not to bend, and Mike to stop dropping his head and closing his eyes. Then she looked up and saw me.

She didn't quite wince. In all the time I'd known her, Danielle Hernandez had never *winced*. But there was a flash of disgust. Perhaps even concern.

"Alright, you two, class is over. Showers or crawl away or whatever it is you do."

One of them, a tawny mustache over a thin, mean sliver of a mouth, pointed at the clock. "We've got five minutes left."

Dani turned a glare on him that had made many a better man quail. "You work for five more minutes, and we're gonna have to find out if the defibrillator they've got in the office works or not."

They both beat a hasty retreat.

"Jesus, Jack. What the hell happened to you?"

"Occupational hazard."

"What, somebody smash a camera into your face while you were getting pictures of them cheating?"

"Nope. He only used his fists. And his head. Maybe a couple elbows."

"You need to get back on the mat, work on your game."

"Well, there were two of them. I gave as good as I got, I promise."

"Lift up your shirt."

"In my vulnerable and compromised state, you'd seek to…"

I caught just the minor of the glare I knew Dani to be capable of. I tugged off the t-shirt. My ribs were a yellow and blue patchwork of bruise, just like my cheeks. My back twisted horribly.

"Goddammit. I've got my kit in my car. Go sit on a bench in an open bathroom and wait."

"Yes, ma'am."

In the bathroom/shower room I pulled a bench that was up against the wall into the middle of the room and sat. Dani came along soon, closing the door behind her. I caught a glance of Nick looking worriedly from down the hallway.

"Uh, Mr. Dixon, I…"

I gave him a smile and a thumbs-up as Dani shut the door.

"This is gonna cost you, Dixon."

"How much?"

She thought a moment. "Beef Wellington."

"Your place or mine?"

"As if you and me and Emily can all dine in your galley."

"Conditions?"

"Grass-fed tenderloin. You *make* the puff pastry. Don't try and pass off any of that freezer case stuff. Ditto the crepes."

I was inclined to fight on the puff pastry, as making that from scratch was a right pain in the ass.

But not as much as the pain in my ribcage and my back. "Done."

She sighed and began unzipping pockets on the duffel bag she'd hauled in from her car.

The resulting examination revealed nothing broken, but plenty bruised. I also passed the concussion protocol. After a few minutes of therapeutic massage during which I proposed marriage only once, she bandaged me up very loosely, really just to hold the ice-packs in place. She handed over a page of instructions—when to change the bandages, some stretches and therapies I could do at home, and finally, a prescription.

"Thanks, doc," I said, as she handed over the scrap of paper.

"Emergencies only, Jack. Muscle relaxers can be habit-forming, just like painkillers. But I don't like the look of those ribs. Exertion could lead to spasms. I don't suppose you'll take it easy for a couple of days."

"No can do. Working."

"What is it?"

"Runaway kid."

"He the one that kicked your ass?"

"No, those were employees of his father. I think."

She frowned. "Aren't missing kids cop stuff?"

"Not if the kid's eighteen and officially dropped out."

"You check the recruitment centers?"

"Called 'em on downtime. So did the principal of the kid's school. No soap."

She sighed. "Okay. When do we get our Wellington?"

"When I'm done, okay? It takes more than two weeks, I'll spring for the wine."

"Better not be Arbor Mist."

"I wouldn't dream of it, Dani."

I slid off the bench and stood, pulled my shirt back on. We shared one of those half-handshakes, half-hugging things. She went easy on me on account of the ribs.

Outside, Nick was hand-wringing. I didn't have time for it, so I just brushed past him while he sputtered at me. Apparently he knew better than to bother Dani, so out we both went. She to her jeep, me to the company car.

"You got a *car*?"

"Company," I said. "And if I don't go check in with the owner of said company, I'm going to be in some deep shit."

"Seems like you're already in deep shit. Try and keep your head above it."

"I always do."

Dani climbed into her jeep, slinging her medical bag into the back of the cab. When she pulled away I got a glimpse of a couple of veteran's organization bumper stickers, and the Combat Action Ribbon version of the Maryland license plate.

Chapter 18

swung by the *Belle* and cleaned myself up before heading into work. In fresh jeans, boots, and a light Henley — it looked like rain and the wind was offering the first taste of fall — I almost felt human again.

I avoided the various temptations offered by Wawa just past the breakfast rush and pulled into an empty spot at the office. When I walked in, Brock was posted up by the door, obviously keeping a look-out for me.

"Boss wants to see you right away," he began. "He's kinda pissed you took so long."

I turned to face him so he could get the full effect of the bruises on my face.

"Crap," he sputtered. "What happened?"

"Disagreement over the limits of corporate hegemony."

I could see the gears whirring behind his eyes as Brock tried to process that number of syllables.

"Couple of toughs working for my missing kid's father tried to work me over."

"You need backup."

"I'm still walking," I said, and I shrugged past him on my way to Jason's office.

I knew my boss was pissed because he didn't offer me any coffee, despite there being a steaming French press full of the good stuff on a sideboard.

He was focused on something on his monitor, didn't even glance at me. "Sit down, Jack," he began in his stern voice.

"Gimme a minute," I said, putting just a touch of a whimper into my voice. "Not moving so well."

"If you're late because you're hungover, that might be a bridge too goddamned far. I put up with your shit because you're a good investigator, but there are limits to how far I'll tolerate somebody building his *mystique* at my expense."

I sighed as I sat down. Nothing for it but to wait for him to turn and face me. Finally, he did, ostentatiously slipping his glasses back down onto his nose.

When he did he blinked a few times as he got a look at my shiner, the bruise on my jaw.

"What the blue hells?"

"Two security guards from the father's office. ADI holdings? They caught up with me in a park in Glasgow."

Jason paused, biting his lips a moment. "Had they, perhaps, some reason to feel offended on their employer's behalf?"

"Hand to God, Jason. I went in, I tried to charm the receptionist. I think she would've listened, too, had she not *already* pressed the panic button. Their response time was professional."

"So they braced you and beat the shit out of you right there in the office? That's rougher than I expect for Wilmington. Office wasn't on 4th Street, was it?"

"Nah, they didn't come right at me there. I dropped a card on the office floor as they walked me out. Kinda thought the receptionist might pick it up, give me a call."

I could see the grin start to spread on his face.

"Don't you dare," I said. "Don't you dare laugh at this."

"She called you, didn't she."

I said nothing. I stared stoically straight ahead.

"She called you. And she brought you to the park with a tremble in her voice and the threat of a tear in her eye."

I kept on staring.

"And you rode in like the dumbest knight that ever strapped on armor, straight into an ass-kicking."

"I kicked a little myself."

"I don't doubt that," my boss said. "But I also know you probably held back."

"Don't start this."

"One day, Jack, you're gonna have to stop doing that. I know you don't like to think you're hurting someone."

"That's hardly a bad thing."

"But it's gonna cost you."

Not as much as not holding back already had, I thought, but did not say.

"Look. I don't know why they came after me. I don't think Gen, the receptionist, I don't think she wanted to do it. She was nervous as hell. I'd even say scared. Maybe they've got some kind of blanket policy about snoops."

"Can't be some kind of custody or visitation thing, right?"

"At this point, the kid is an adult, so none of that's in play. He can go see the dad whenever he wants."

"Dad snatch him up for some reason?"

"I don't get the sense that dad is super aware of the kid's existence."

"Guilty conscience."

"He works for a capital investment firm. He's got every reason to have one."

"Find anything useful at the school?"

"Maybe. Kid who knows him real well. I think she's very likely the kind who'll hear from him eventually. Or think of something."

I could see him tap a few keys, likely bringing up the case file. "Liza?"

"Elizabeth Mortimer-Hanes will be her name in the file. But yeah, Liza."

"Got her phone number?"

"She's a minor, Jason. I can't go question her. But I can wait for her to come to me."

"Fair. What about this Gen? Got her info."

"I've got her phone number on a card."

"Think she'll pick up?"

"I have my doubts but I'll give it a shot."

I fished the card from my wallet, took out my phone, and dialed it. No answer. The voicemail message I'd heard yesterday played again. I hung up before the beep.

While I was dialing, Jason had been tapping away. One of the screens on the wall behind him lit up with a LinkedIn profile. The other, a Facebook page.

He pointed. From the Facebook page, Gen—with more makeup than she'd worn in the office, but extremely well done around her eyes—stared back from a selfie, with some blurry forms behind her.

According to the LinkedIn page, her name was Geneva Lawton and she was an administrative professional with eighteen months' experience. She was a student at University of Delaware, enrolled in a BA-to-MBA program.

"Let me see the card," Jason said. I handed it over. He held it up to his monitor and looked. "Different number on her resume."

"Probably a work phone, then."

"Worth a shot," I said. "Give me the other number."

He wrote it down. I dialed it.

Second ring picked up. A hushed, "Hello?"

"Geneva."

"Who is this?"

I cleared my throat. "Jack Dixon."

Dead silence. "Who?"

"The guy whose bone structure your pals tried to rearrange yesterday afternoon."

"Can't talk about this now. Call me after five," she said all in a rush, and then hung up.

I looked up to Jason. "Progress. Instruction to call her after five."

He jerked his head toward the coffee. "Pour yourself some, then go build out the case file as much as you can. See what ADI holdings does. Show Brock how to do research."

"Do I have to?"

"You don't have to pour yourself any coffee."

Chapter 19

Case files don't build themselves, but having to teach a guy like Brock Diamante to make one, how to fill it out, how to make sure all the tags were correct, that the people who were connected to each other were connected in our files, that took some doing.

I had organized two major headings: family and school. In school I labeled Liza and Dr. Thalheim as people of interest. On the latter, I wasn't entirely sure why. I didn't like him, and I was listening to my gut. I glanced over at Brock, who wore something he probably called a "chronometer" at least the size of a salad plate on his wrist. His was some kind of black anodized material and didn't look to be in the same class as Dr. Thalheim's.

"Hey, Brock. Are you a watch guy?"

"Huh?"

"Watches. You collect them, find them interesting?"

"Well, I wouldn't say I collect 'em, but yeah, I like to have a nice timepiece. This one is a Divemaster, rated…"

I held up a hand. Blessed silence fell. The boy wanted to learn, I'd give him that.

"I don't care. What I do care to know is, if you saw a watch, an expensive one, could you identify it?"

"I'm not a watch encyclopedia."

"I mean if you saw it, and you had some time to research it, could you narrow it down?"

"You got a side job looking for a missing watch?"

"Sure," I said flatly. "Big, rich blue face, leather band. It looked expensive, but maybe it was just a fifty-dollar job from Sears."

"You see a marque on it anywhere?"

"Are you asking me if it was tarnished?"

"No, like a maker's symbol. See, this here is…" He started to show me his chrono-dive or whatever it was. I waved it away.

"I think so. Some letters. I-W-something."

"IWC?"

"I think that was it, yeah."

Brock frowned and waved me away from the keyboard. He opened up a new tab. "What color was it?"

"Blue face, like I said. Leather band."

He typed a few times. Opened up an image and showed it to me. "Something like this?"

"That looks like the one, or at least very close," I said, leaning in.

"That is an IWC Portugieser Automatic. It is not cheap."

"How much is not cheap?"

"About twelve grand, maybe thirteen."

I sat bolt upright in my chair. "People pay *twelve thousand dollars* for a watch?"

He shrugged. "It's a statement piece."

"Gimme back the keyboard." I did some rudimentary checking on the money a school psychiatrist or counselor or psychologist could earn. Most of the data was taken from public schools, of course, and Farrington's tuition was high.

Still, I didn't see any reason why Dr. Thalheim should be wearing a twelve thousand-dollar watch.

"Why do you care so much about a watch, anyway?"

"Guy wearing it should…maybe not be able to afford it."

"You can finance them," Brock pointed out.

"Finance a watch?"

He nodded.

I made a note in the file about looking at Thalheim's financial situation if it was in any way possible short of stealing his mail or breaking and entering.

At that point, my phone rang. The caller was identified as Cecil County Sheriff's Department.

I was tired. I was still sore. I was angry at myself for making no headway on the case. So I assayed a joke.

"Finally decided to check in with a professional?"

"You need to find a day job so you can make sure not to quit it, Jack."

I'd lucked out. It was Bob. "Maybe you're just not my target audience."

A sigh. "How's the Kennelly case?"

"I'm developing promising leads."

"Don't fuck around on this. I'm old friends with Susan. She might not be bothering you because she doesn't want to throw you off, but she's calling me two, three times a day asking if I've heard anything."

"Well, maybe you can answer some questions about the dad."

"Maybe. Are you working the case tomorrow night?"

"Why, Corporal Sanderson, are you asking me out?"

"I'm asking if you want to make some money."

"Oh, Bob, tell me this isn't some bouncer job."

"Just one of those barn parties, you know, out in the country? Got a temp liquor license, want a couple of tough looking guys to stand at the door. Could be a couple of hundred bucks."

"Just looking tough and checking IDs, yeah?"

"No big deal. Just a bunch of kids getting a little rowdy on a Friday."

"Lot of these kids got gun-racks on their trucks, Bob."

"No firearms. Party organizers were very clear about that."

"Fine. Pick me up?"

"Eight p.m. Wear a black t-shirt. And for Chrissakes, try to look tough."

He hung up. A few moments later I got a text with an address in it. Google Maps told me it was well out in the woods, practically the Pennsylvania line. Thankfully Bob was driving.

"Can you get me a gig like that?" Brock had, evidently, been listening.

"If Bob asks me to recommend somebody, maybe. But he usually only asks me when he doesn't have anybody else." Or when he suspects I've got less than five hundred bucks to my name. Which was far more often than I'd like to admit.

"Fine. We done with the case list?"

"Almost. But we do have some more hands-on work later."

"What's that?"

"Detecting and then evading potential surveillance. Surveilling in turn. Watching a partner discreetly while they make contact with a person of interest."

"Oh, thank god, we get to leave the office. I'll drive."

"Not until we get where we're going, you won't."

"You're not driving my car."

"Neither are you, Brock. Neon orange accents and loud engines stick out like a fart in a champagne glass. We want to be just another little bubble."

We whiled away a few more hours, got in on the office lunch order—I did a salad with chicken, hold the dressing, and everyone made their jokes. While I miserably forked romaine and red onion and radish into my mouth, Brock messily devoured a burger, mozzarella sticks, and fries. None of it looked particularly good on its own, but compared to a double handful of undressed greens and a block of vulcanized chicken breast, it looked like ambrosia.

"The salads from this place are notoriously terrible," one of the other break room occupants said as he dug into pasta.

"Salads are always terrible. Unless you suddenly add enough cheese and mayonnaise and protein and throw out half the lettuce and stick it on a sub roll."

"Then why do you eat it?" Brock said. "Why not order something good?"

The correct answer was that nothing from the local pizzeria, except the pizza, was good. Pizza was *always* good. What I went with was a little less combative.

"I eat less at lunch so I can eat more at dinner."

"Just run more."

"Not everyone's metabolism is as blessed as yours is, Brock."

He shrugged. Our pasta-slurping coworker muttered that I'd know the menus better if I came into the office more.

"But then," I said, "I'd be forced to endure your company, Matt."

"Why is it you get all these special privileges anyway?" Brock had finished his burger, his mozzarella sticks, and his fries, and was now hunting around in the bag for stray crumbs of fried anything.

"That's between me and the boss. Let's say I don't do well on land or in group situations."

I finished what I could stand of my salad and stood. "I'm going to go do some research."

Research, in this case, meant throwing the remains of the greens and chicken into the stand of trees out back of the office and taking a bit of a walk around.

People. They just rubbed me the wrong way. Even someone like Brock, who was just a big damn hound dog that wanted to help and was too dumb to figure out how.

A few circuits of the building and I was back at it in front of the computer. I tried to narrow the scope of Thalheim's likely income a little further. Seemed like he also had a private practice. In fact, it was possible he was simply contracted to the school from his practice.

This was probably nothing; that school cost an absurd amount of money and they probably used a not inconsiderable amount of it to pay him. Factor in family money, good investment, private practice, who knew what he might have socked away?

I also researched watches, looking at that model and others like it. None of them seemed to come in south of ten grand, unless they were a deliberate knockoff or purchased in poor condition and refurbished.

Dr. Thalheim did not seem like the type to spend his weekends hunched over a worktable, wearing magnifying glasses, and carefully cleaning tiny, easily broken watch parts.

I went pretty far down the rabbit hole. Once I realized that I was internalizing the difference between a tourbillon and a chronometer I had to pull the plug.

It would not do to become a Watch Guy. I had a low-cost aesthetic to maintain. I still had a couple of hours before I could call Gen, so I spun back to the *Belle* to grab an early dinner. I went digging in the cabinets to find a fresh jar of my staff of life.

This one had sesame seeds and dried cranberries in it, and had it over the whey-protein stuff in spades. I limited myself to a healthy two spoonfuls, slid the jar into the fridge, and drove slowly back to the office.

Once there, I dialed Gen's personal number. It was five-oh-two. I hoped I didn't look desperate.

It went a few rings and I thought I was getting the runaround. Then a voice picked up. A voice a little less scared than earlier that day.

"Jack?"

"Maybe we ought to stick with Mr. Dixon until you don't lure me into a beating."

"I didn't want to do that," she said. Suddenly her voice had a little

more spirit in it. "You don't have to believe that if you don't want to. I can't make you. But I didn't get a choice."

People always said that when what they meant was *I made a choice that made life easier for me, regardless of what it did to anyone else.*

I didn't share that thought with her. Moral philosophy, while interesting, rarely got an investigator anywhere much in an interview.

"Fine. Where do you want to meet?"

"One of the bars in Trolley Square?"

"That's a little far for me," I said. "How about one of the strip malls along 40 in Glasgow or Bear? Plenty of bars there."

"I want a crowd," she said. "How about Main Street in Newark? Lots of places there."

"You can blend there. Anyone looking for me is gonna have no trouble."

"Nobody will be looking for you. I promise."

"Fine." I sighed. "Where?"

"Finn McCool's," she said.

"Fine. I'll be there. Seven."

"Okay." A pause. "And I am sorry. I didn't think they'd actually try to…hurt you."

"Sure." We hung up.

I went inside and gave the kind of low-key guy-to-guy nod to Brock that would let him know it was time to go.

"You drive," I said. "But we're still taking the company car."

"Boss says I'm not allowed to take a company car."

"Well, how's he gonna find out?" I tossed him the keys.

He shrugged and got in.

Chapter 20

Halfway up 279 into Newark, I knew exactly why Jason didn't want Brock behind the wheel of any company cars, and he was right. He was wise and knowing, and I was a fool for having second-guessed him and contravened his commandments.

"Brock," I said, fighting for calm control of my voice.

"Yeah?"

"Let's stay within twenty of what's posted."

"Oh, don't worry about the cops, I got friends."

"I'm not worried about the cops. I'm worried that my last meal is gonna be fourteen inches of telephone pole."

"Oh." He eased off a little, and my stomach settled back into *detente* with the coffee and peanut butter that filled it. "You should take the defensive driving course. I've taken it twice. It really—"

"Brock. Does taking the course require a car?"

"Well, yeah, you have to learn on a car you know well first."

I went silent and let him work out the problem for himself. When we neared one of the public parking lots I directed him into it.

It was September, UD was in session, and the weather was good. The bars and the restaurants were going to be full. We were fairly lucky to find a public spot just before a big Thursday night out started up. Even at just past six, students crowded the sidewalks. The air was still just warm enough that muscle shirts, bare-midriff tops, and very small shorts were the order of the day. And my erstwhile partner had noticed that.

I poked him in the ribs.

"We ain't here to pick up co-eds, kid. Or even to watch them. Pay attention."

"To what?"

"Anybody who looks out of place. Anybody who looks like they're watching me and the person I'm meeting instead of their own date or friends." I decided to quickly amend that. "Some guys…maybe some girls, too…will look at her because. Well, because. But I'm trusting you to figure out the difference."

"What if somebody's checking *you* out."

"We deal in trying to uncover realities, which means stripping away delusions, Brock."

He snorted. "Okay, so where am I going?"

"Preferably a bar across the street with outdoor seating. I'll get the same for me and Gen if I can. If I can't, you find a reason to linger on the street just outside our bar—buy a burrito and sit on a wall or a bench or something. Eat—or drink—slowly. If you think an emergency is imminent, do what you have to do."

"Uh, how blank of a check are you writing me, here? And what's my food budget?"

"Don't commit any felonies unless they're committed at you first. And the firm should reimburse you for any honest expenditures. If you have more than one drink, though, you're gonna be explaining yourself to Jason."

"He has had more than one drink in a workday."

"His name is on the door. You're the most recent hire."

He nodded. "Wait a few minutes here. We don't want to be seen walking along the street together."

I went out ahead of him. The crowd was bustling. If I was in any kind of hurry, I could've worked up a pretty solid and righteous anger over how no one had any damn spatial awareness. They walked slowly, drifting apart from one another as they chatted and looked at their phones. They stopped dead when a tweet or a snap caught their attention.

Naturally, I was the very picture of grace, poise, and total situational awareness. Several college students were saved the indignity of bouncing into the street off my chest or my elbow only by my constant awareness of my own physical presence, and the space I occupied.

"Careful," I murmured to myself. "Keep thinking this way and you'll be a grumpy old asshole complaining about the kids for the rest of your life. The kids have many sterling qualities."

Name two.

I ignored that thought and scoped the outside of Finn McCool's. There were outdoor tables, though nothing too good across the street. I hoped Brock could improvise.

I walked on for a few blocks past the meeting spot. While I had to admit that a crowd of college students offered its diversions, I manfully ignored them and spent the time casing the place.

I certainly stood out. While there were no shortage of bearded men with short hair in tight single colored t-shirts, most of them had tattoos up and down their arms, and mine were bare as far as they could be seen. Moreover, I was clearly at least a few years older than the crowd, not walking with a group, not wearing headphones.

I made it more or less to the end of the commercial part of Main, crossed the street, and started down the other side. I figured Gen would be coming down from Wilmington, which probably meant I-95 to Route 273, which became Main Street. Which meant she'd be coming at me to get to Finn McCool's. I saw nothing unusual. By which I meant I didn't see anyone wearing a suit jacket that had been modified for a man with no neck and a weapon on his belt.

I crossed back at a crosswalk, grabbed a spot of wall and leaned against it, pulled out my phone. I reflected on the fact that, in a movie or a novel, the PI would be reading the paper and probably smoking a pipe while he waited. I wondered when was the last time I'd even bought a paper.

I kept one eye on the baseball scores on my phone, and the other on the cars that passed.

I caught a glimpse of her, leaning forward over the steering wheel of a blue-green Honda Fit, looking for parking. She turned right, down a cross street that would put her in a public lot just a short walk from the street.

I decided to take a bit of a bold approach, though it would mean Brock would lose me. If, indeed, he had me. I didn't want to be obvious about looking for him, so I just walked off after her car.

As I got there, I saw Gen walking toward the exit, looking down at her phone. I put myself right in her path and didn't move. She did, though, catching herself just before I would've filled up her field of vision. She looked up, let out a soft "Oh." Then, "You."

"Me." I fought the urge to snatch the phone out of her hand to see if she was sending a text or any other kind of message to someone. I didn't.

She wore slim fitted black slacks and a sleeveless purple blouse. Her bare arms were toned, and — helping her fit right in — sported a small handful of tastefully inked tattoos. The quality of the work looked good and I definitely felt like I could spend considerable time examining them. I pulled my eyes back to hers. Still large, still brown. Despite the previous day's unpleasantness, I still liked looking at them.

"I thought you'd be waiting for me at the bar. Grabbing a table, scoping the place out."

"Already did," I said. "The second part, anyway. This way I get to see if you arrived with anyone who's going to try and do violence to me again."

"Well," she said, "I didn't. And now, if you're going to walk me to the bar, walk me to the bar." She shifted her bag and the jacket that matched her slacks to her other hand.

I felt, suddenly, not entirely in command of the situation. While I had several inches on her in height, I didn't really have to change my stride to walk beside her; she took long yet precise steps, in heels no less.

"Find the place okay?"

"Everyone who's lived around here can find a place on Main Street," Gen said.

"Did you go to UD?"

She shook her head. "Not for undergrad, not right away. Out-of-state tuition. No dice. Had to do community college first, save some money. Now I do, but as a commuter/online student." I knew this stuff already, but it was good to hear her telling me the truth.

"Better than going into debt."

"You're not kidding," she said.

I was starting to feel too relaxed with her. Thankfully, we reached the bar. I let her up the stairs first. Ever the gentleman, I kept my eyes dutifully on the steps at my feet and did not inspect the fit of her slacks.

"Let's sit outside," I said. I gestured to a table and she cocked an eyebrow at me.

"Shouldn't you ask the hostess?"

"Sure. What would you like to drink?"

"Smithwick's," she said. She quickly dug in her purse and came out with a twenty. "And it's on me, since I asked for the meeting."

I took the bill and gave her a salute, and more of a charming smile—maybe as high as number five—than I thought she deserved. I reminded myself that this was the woman who tried to set me up earlier.

Once inside, I turned the smile on full, the whole number twelve, and handed the folded twenty over to the hostess. "Took a table outside. Hope that's all right." I brushed right past her before she could say if it was or wasn't and went to the bar.

Yes, I was circumventing the service industry, but there was a chance I'd know the bartender. There was usually a chance I'd know the bartender.

I didn't; it was all new-looking college kids. Thankfully they weren't crowded yet. Ordering caused me to pause a moment. I generally avoided beer on weeknights, but I couldn't start putting whiskey away, and to be perfectly honest, I've never liked the Irish whiskey all that much and that was most of what they had. So in a few moments I was back outside, having carried a pint each of Guinness and Smithwick's past the speechless hostess.

I set Gen's beer down in front of her and hooked the spare seat with my foot, dragging it to a spot where I could see the crowd.

"So," I said, setting her change carefully down on the wrought-iron table. "Why are we here?"

"To enjoy the evening air with a fine beverage?" Her voice was a little taunting, a little throaty. I felt something in my chest flutter. Couldn't be the heart.

"I think we've got some business to do before there's any enjoying to be done." I watched the Guinness settle along the side of the glass, one of the small miracles of the world that managed to never get old.

"Fair. I am sorry for calling you in. I thought they would… warn you off or something." I looked at her, trying to judge her sincerity. Either she was a theater minor or she meant it. Part of it, at least.

With one of her fingers she gestured at the bruise under my eye. "Is that…is it bad? It hurt?" Her fingertip brushed it.

"Not as bad as the probably broken ribs or the back spasms," I said. "Why did those two jackals even want to threaten me, much less beat me? All I did was walk in to the office."

"And show them up, and drop a PI's card with a number written on it, and evade their attempt to trespass you."

"Details."

"Look, Mr. Kennelly has been the target of some media inquiries lately, and some people are threatening legal action. Maybe they thought you'd been hired by them."

"Well, I think I'd have a case. What does Mr. Kennelly *do*, anyway?"

"He manages ADI holdings, which manages several companies."

"What does that actually mean?"

Gen dropped her eyes and drank her beer. It was no tiny, old fashioned ladylike sip, either. I appreciated that. "It means he comes from old money, and he moves it around into different companies, then cashes out once it looks like work."

Interesting. I could definitely get somewhere with this. "I don't care what companies he's run into the ground or who is threatening to sue him. I just want to find his son. Be nice if he did, too."

"He probably does, but he…he lives a very insulated life. I work for him, and I don't think I know him."

"What do you do for him?"

"Manage the phones, his calendar and appointments, pay his personal and company bills—just the ADI bills, not all the companies it holds. Which is part of why I called."

She dug into her purse again. "I can't show you the entire records, but Mr. Kennelly's insurance plan started getting odd claims about a week before Gabriel's disappearance. Maybe it's nothing. But I've never heard of the company that's billing it."

She held out a billing statement. Much of it had been blacked out, professionally, it looked like.

The unredacted portions listed a company called "Ladders" and billing amounts for "services" and "therapies."

"Ladders?"

"No idea what they do, but it's expensive."

"Contact info?"

"I found a phone number, but I don't think it's manned. Goes straight to a mailbox. Doesn't identify itself."

She was about halfway through her beer, beating me considerably. But I had two speeds when it came to beer: slow and gulp. I was keeping it in first gear.

"Area code?"

"Maryland, 443."

I took a slightly larger swallow of my beer. A feeling was growing in the pit of my stomach. A feeling I didn't like. It must've showed on my face, because Gen's hand landed on my arm.

"You okay, Mr. Dixon?"

"Jack," I said, shaking myself out of it. "And…yeah. Just trying to make an intuitive leap I don't have enough information for yet. Can I keep this?" I gestured with the insurance billing statement.

"Sure."

"Why wouldn't his insurer try and contest payments from a sketchy provider?"

She laughed lightly, revealing even, bright teeth. "He pays his insurance company more a month than he pays me, even counting my tuition disbursement. They cover everything."

"Must be nice," I murmured, thinking of Dani. Who was, for all intents and purposes, my insurance plan *and* my primary care doc *and* my specialist referral.

"We can't all be born rich," Gen said.

"Look," I said, setting the paper down and fixing her with a concerned and serious expression. It certainly grabbed all of her attention. She ran a hand against the side of her hair, smoothing it down. Not that it needed it. "If you hear anything more from this company, or anything connects it to Gabriel, call me."

"I will."

I threw back the rest of my Guinness. "I've got to go. Before I do, why'd you even call them, the other morning."

"A big man bursts into my office with his arms and shoulders barely fitting in his off the rack jacket, wanting to ask me questions about my boss, and you wonder why I was afraid?"

"That's fair," I said. "I could've finessed that approach a little more."

"It's all right," she said, meeting my eyes evenly, smiling just a tiny bit. "I shouldn't have been scared. I'm not scared now."

"Good," I said. "Call me if you hear anything?"

"Vice versa," she said, standing as I did, lifting her glass and finishing the dark red ale in one motion.

"Will do," I agreed.

We walked down the stairs.

"Walk me back to my car?"

I am nothing if not a gentleman.

* * *

I found Brock with the litter of a burrito, three tacos, and a bag of chips with guac from the local mission burrito place around him.

"Looks like an eventful contact," he said.

"Yep."

"Get anything actionable?"

"Maybe."

"Got her number?"

"Already had it."

"Can I have it?"

"You want to walk back to the office?"

Chapter 21

"Ladders," Jason said, with just a hint of a question.

"Ladders," I confirmed. "Some kind of healthcare provider. Without a website, monitored email, or address that we know about."

"We can check the databases, find out who registered the company." He tapped the paper. "What does 'therapy' and 'services' being broken down into separate charges make you think?"

"That it's some kind of residential deal. Charge for both ends of it."

"Well, there's no hospital or retreat around here called Ladders."

"That we know of. Could be a practice located inside one of the hospitals. But…"

"I doubt it," we both said, echoing one another. He gestured for me to continue. "More likely than that, it's some kind of exclusive place. It's more expensive than the average. I checked that already."

"Hm. Alright, well, let's see if we can find the filings, figure out who's behind this."

I sat back in the chair, winced as my ribs reminded me they were damaged. "Could be that Mr. Kennelly's been shipped off to get the Blue Demons chased away."

"But you don't think so."

I shook my head. "I really don't."

He tapped away at his keyboard. "Ladders. Entity created in Maryland, just under a year ago. Registered by some law firm down in Harford County. Fitzgerald and Urden."

"I go down there, they're just gonna say 'privilege.'"

"There are more old-fashioned ways."

"I'm not B&Eing a law firm, even a sketchy one that just sets up corporations on behalf of even more suspect clients."

"You are overburdened by conscience, Jack."

"Well," I said, casting about for ideas. "I'm working the door for a party up in the woods tomorrow night. I could ask around there. Can't stay hidden forever."

"Yeah, definitely ask a bunch of kids if they've heard of some fly by night healthcare service provider."

"Look, if we even find an address, I'll go knock on the door. Happily. But until then, it's just a name. Might be some registries we can search to attach the phone number to a physical address."

"Yeah, we're on those databases. Get on it, then." I made my way to the door and he stopped me with a drawn out, "You know…"

I waited, hand on the handle.

"You're supposed to get permission to do those kind of security jobs while you're on the clock for me."

"I'm supposed to do a lot of things. Go to church. Call my folks. Cardio. Avoid the demon drink."

"Just go do some research."

Chapter 22

I once again slipped into my neighbor's wifi in order to research into the early evening. At least now I had a cocktail to while away the time. Of course, that cocktail was nothing more than a generous pour from a new bottle of rye over a couple dense cubes of ice. I had idly thought about filling the prescription Dani'd written me while I walked home—Brock had taken me halfway, and then I'd just wanted to breathe the night air. But I couldn't afford to be taking muscle relaxers unless the pain got so bad that I couldn't walk. And even then I'd think twice about it.

I did manage, through diligent battering of ancient and creaky state databases and info-lookup subscriptions the firm maintained, to find an address for Ladders.

"A goddamn PO Box." I had a momentary urge to hurl my laptop into the water. Like most of my impulses, it would've felt good, but hindered investigative progress.

I decided to try and investigate ADI holdings. Not much turned up on Mr. Kennelly, as I already knew. His company, on the other hand, had made some waves. Seems they'd tried buying some local restaurants and ridden them straight into the ground. Done it through other companies, of course, but some local journalists had managed to trail it back to him.

"Pretty small-time shit to roust people over. Maybe I'd just scared Gen."

My thoughts had included a lot of her on my walk home. She was at least half the reason for the extra fingers of rye in my glass. I took a sip, seeking its counsel.

"I'm getting played, right?" I said aloud. One of the night birds around the marina yelled at me. "I'm getting played," I answered myself.

"But then again." I paused. Some cats yowled. I wanted to yell back at them, but I figured I was just jealous that somebody, somewhere, was enjoying themselves. "I'm probably getting played, *but just in case* I better make sure to keep in touch with her." I settled on that and knocked back the rest of my drink. I looked at the bottle, fresh and new promising joy.

"It's medicinal," I said as I poured a second. To my nightly peanut butter and apple I'd added a carrot, for ballast. Me and the rye went back and forth and came up with a plan of action for the next day.

Chapter 23

The next morning, I found myself outside a post office just over the Susquehanna in Harford County, having navigated via bus, a bit of walking, and a Lyft. I'd have to expense the last part, and I was a little leery of burdening Ms. Kennelly with that.

But I found myself inside and waiting in line in the unnecessary AC. Once I got to the window, a woman with a nametag reading Marianne greeted me with that efficient, slightly bored manner I've always felt the best government employees affected.

"Hi. Who would I talk to about a PO box?"

She gestured to the window next to her, which was vacant, and picked up a phone. "George, someone for a PO Box."

It took a few minutes for George to wander up. He'd seen better days. His USPS polo strained against a pot belly. His nametag and the ID badge on the lanyard around his neck were so yellowed by cigarette smoke that I don't think I could've read them. His nails were similarly yellowed. The wisps of hair that clung to his shiny, sweaty skull were off-white.

"Cost is $40 a year, renewable automatically but nonrefundable," George wheezed. He stopped in the middle of reaching for the paperwork to surrender to smoker's cough.

"George," I said, leaning conspiratorially over, "you want to head outside, get some fresh air, discuss it there? Maybe catch a smoke?"

He nodded yes through his coughing, snatching papers and a clipboard. He pointed to the front door, then to the left, indicating I should meet him there. I gave Marianne, who looked a little disgusted, a little wave and went back out into the just-warm day.

George was already lighting up when I got out there.

"Can you believe how expensive those things are getting these days," I began, gesturing to the pack of Camels he was slipping back into his pocket.

He plucked the cigarette out of his mouth and ashed away the tip. "Fuckin' state wanted to get in on it, right? Tax revenue, man. All they want."

I didn't particularly want to get into a debate about the pros and cons of consumption taxes with George, but I thought I could string him along a bit.

"Hell, probably part of their plan all along. So many guys I knew in the Navy learned to smoke and dip there. Now they're being hounded to quit and paying extra for the habit Uncle Sam taught 'em."

"Navy, huh? I was Air Force. When I started," he rasped, "you could either spend breaks reading the fuckin' handbook, or you could smoke. Who'd choose the book?"

Me, I thought. I had my vices, but tobacco had never been one of them.

"Gets you comin' and goin', huh?" George nodded and laughed. I reached into my pocket and came out with some green showing between thumb and forefinger. "Look George, let me level with you. I don't want a PO box."

"I ain't committing no mail fraud, and I ain't giving you a look at anyone's mail," he sputtered, suddenly going pale. He flicked away his cigarette and started to walk away. I shuffled a couple steps to stay in front of him. On footspeed alone, I was pretty sure I could play man defense on George all day if I had to.

"Whoa, buddy. Whoa. Nothing like that. I don't want you to break any laws." At least I didn't think so. I wasn't entirely sure. "There's a PO box in there. I want you to let me know how often it gets emptied, and if you can, by who. That's all."

"Whaddya mean, by who?"

I shrugged. "Describe the person for me. Get a license plate if you happen to catch a smoke out here. That's all."

"And for what?"

"Camel money?" I let more of the edge of the twenty slip out between my fingers. "All you have to do is text me."

He looked at the money and was reaching for it. Suddenly a head peaked around the corner. Marianne, scowling.

George turned and scurried around the back. I smiled at Marianne and walked away.

I cursed all the way back over the Tydings Bridge.

Chapter 24

I was on the bus when my phone started buzzing.

"Hello, Ms. Kennelly," I said.

"Mr. Dixon." A deep breath. "Are you getting anywhere?"

"I'm developing leads, ma'am."

"Anything promising?"

I sighed. "I don't want to get your hopes up by sharing something that turns out to be fruitless."

The bus made a loud wheezing sound as it took a turn, the tires and brakes screeching.

"What's that noise? Are you driving?"

"No, ma'am. On a bus."

There was silence on the other end of the line. I seized on it. "Ms. Kennelly, is there any chance of getting Gabriel's father to speak with me? I can't seem to get ahold of him." Telling her that his building's security goons seemed determined to beat my head in just for coming to his office didn't seem like a winning play.

"That man lives in a state of perpetual paranoia. Everyone is out to get him, or his money, which in his mind are one and the same."

"I see. Do you think that could be related to Gabriel's disappearance?"

A sigh. "Running away to get dad's attention? It's not impossible, but Gabriel learned a long time ago to do without that. Don't see what would suddenly change for him."

"I have another question. Does the name 'Ladders' mean anything to you? As a company, maybe a healthcare provider?

"I can't say it does. Sounds like a place the depraved rich would go for a few weeks to dry out."

"It does, at that." I adjusted my seat and tried to avoid letting a heavy breath into the phone when my ribs reminded me that they had indeed been drummed upon. "Ms. Kennelly, one way or another, I'll have a report for you on Monday."

"One way or another? I don't like the sound of that."

"Ms. Kennelly, I'm going to find Gabriel." *Oh God damnit.* I had to say that out loud, to the client, didn't I?

"I like your confidence, Mr. Dixon. But I don't know if I believe it."

That'd make two of us. "Nothing's shaken it so far, Ms. Kennelly." If you're gonna tell one lie, you might as well compound it.

"Fine. I have to go back to work. Please keep me updated."

"Of course."

We hung up, and I tried to find a comfortable way to sit on a Cecil Transit Bus with bad ribs and a bad back and a sour stomach from not enough food and too much whiskey the night before.

Not only could I not find a missing kid, I couldn't find that, either.

Chapter 25

The rest of the day passed uneventfully. The fall of evening found me trying to choose between a plain back t-shirt that was just a bit *too* tight and one that had some nerd decorations just under the collar—a golden dragon on the right, a sword on the left. I decided on plain because I didn't want to deal with Bob calling me a nerd all night.

I stuck a small Maglite and a couple of Sharpies in the pockets of my jeans, along with a pocket knife, and wandered out into the parking lot.

Bob pulled up in an unmarked SUV that still screamed cop, with the light panels in the front and back windows and the whipcord antenna on the top.

I hoped the dark would hide my face, but there was no hiding the extra grunt I made as I climbed up into the car. And for all his faults, Bob was still a cop, and that meant he was observant and curious, by training if not by nature.

"What the hell happened to your face?"

"Occupational hazard."

"Making any progress finding the kid?"

"I don't know." I knew he'd keep circling around to find out everything he wanted to know, so I just laid it all out as we drove. The school, the standoffish kids—excepting Liza, whom I didn't mention by name—the doctor I didn't like. I told him about the dad's office and getting roughed up by the security. He stopped me there.

"You let one of them have a face full of LEO-grade pepper spray?"

"Mouthful, too."

"That may not have been super legal, Jack."

"Self-defense."

"At least you didn't shoot him."

"Can't shoot anybody if you don't carry a gun."

"Don't come at me with disarm or disband the police."

I held up a hand. "Come on, Bob. We both know you haven't got another way to feed your kids, and I've seen how much they eat."

"Very funny." He took a turn. We were on some rural highway now. I hadn't paid too much attention. I could tell he was thinking, though, worrying at something.

"You don't like that school doctor for this, do you?"

"I think he's probably an asshole, but how many of those do we run into a day?"

"Still. You didn't like him. That's a gut reaction."

"So is eating at McDonald's," I said. "Doesn't make it material."

"If I were you, I'd go back into that school when they didn't know I was coming. Say I had some follow-up questions, talk to everybody you already talked to."

"I've heard worse ideas. I can do that on Monday, I don't get anywhere else this weekend."

"Hang on. I need to note the date and time." Ostentatiously—and since we were at a stop sign, Bob pulled his phone off the console. He opened up a voice recording app.

"Friday, September 19. Jack Dixon admits an officer of the law had a good idea."

"Very funny. We there yet?"

We were, in fact, just two turns and a long run down a gravel road away, so it was just a few minutes. The gravel road became an uneven mixture of gravel and grass as a large barn rose in the distance. It was strung on all sides with white Christmas lights. From the hayloft the glare of the lights inside was visible. Bob and I walked up together. I was a big guy, and I took up my fair share of space, but I always felt pretty small next to Corporal Sanderson.

As we walked up, gravel crunching under our boots, Bob muttered at me. "Charles is gonna pay us well for this, so…just try and remember that." I wasn't sure why we were getting that warning until I heard an exaggeratedly enthusiastic "Corporal Sanderson!" from near the open cut-out door of the barn.

Charles was my age and trying so very hard to look younger that it exhausted me almost immediately. He wore expensive jeans, cowboy boots, a designer woven belt, and a half-tucked in dress shirt striped vertically and thin in blue, yellow, red, orange, and green. He had sunglasses turned around so the lenses rested on the back of his neck, and a blue trilby with a gray band sitting back on a balding head.

I hated every single thing about him from the moment I clapped eyes on him. This was, to be fair, not an unusual reaction for me.

He and Bob shook hands, Chuck's hand practically disappearing in Bob's giant meathook. Then it was my turn.

"You must be Jack!" I could hear the exclamation points in everything he said as he took my hand. I expected a clammy, floppy handshake and was mildly surprised to find it was neither.

"Bob speaks highly of you," he said. "Says you were some shit-hot wrestler, MMA training and all that." With the back of his hand he gave me what he must've thought was a playful slap in the stomach.

I tried to swallow the resulting scream and it came out as more of a strangled laugh. He made to do it again and I caught his wrist with my hand. I was mad enough from the pain in my ribs to think about turning his wrist to get him under control and then putting him on his back when Bob clapped us both on the shoulder and pulled me away from him.

It was like getting dragged backward by some kind of horrifying industrial clamping robot.

"Better show us where to set up, get us lights, stools, all that."

Charles was eager to smooth over whatever weirdness had just happened that he couldn't parse. His braying, nasal voice haunted me all the rest of the way up the path.

"Hundreds of folks tonight, all to have a good time. Should be no problems. No problems at all. But you know how these things are, gotta have a couple of tough guys working the door."

It was all pretty standard stuff and I tuned him out. I did find myself wishing for a chance to shine my Maglite in Charles' eyes, just to see how badly dilated his pupils were.

He got us situated on some stools. Bob produced a pair of clickers we could put in our fists.

"Three-fifty, that's the Fire Marshal's limit," Charles was saying. "So make sure you're keeping up with that. 'Course, we got all this outdoor space too."

"Bathrooms inside, or…" That was Bob, always on the details.

Charles jerked a thumb around one side of the barn. "Bank of porta johns that way. Get you guys anything? Coffee, water?"

I wanted a beer, but protocol dictated total sobriety. Protocol always dictated things I hated.

"I'll take a coffee," Bob said.

I held up two fingers to indicate a second, and Charles skittered away.

Inside, I heard the DJ testing the sound system with something that combined drum machine, soulless electrified banjo, and a white guy rapping.

"Gonna be a long night," I murmured.

* * *

The first few minutes of door work are always a bit of a fumble. You search for the rhythm. Check the ID with the Maglite, take the money or ticket if you're doing that, put the wristband on, click the attendance counter. It's a lot of small tasks that all have to be done pretty precisely. Thankfully Bob and I weren't managing the money, just checking IDs, strictly twenty-one and over at Charlie's Barn Bash, or whatever this nonsense was called. Then we were taking red Sharpies and drawing a thick X on the back of the hand to show that the person could be served. We also were given white wristbands for voluntary designated drivers. No X for them, and complementary water or soft drinks all night.

Didn't give out a lot of white wristbands, but there were a few.

I confiscated two fake IDs because one was named "Giancarlo Jeter" and the kid was dumb enough to be wearing a Yankees hat. The second was an obvious fake that fell apart from the sweating hand of the kid holding it. When the picture rubbed off on his thumb as he handed it over, he just turned and legged it. I glanced over at Bob, who'd looked up only once he heard fast footsteps, lost in his own work pattern.

"We running people down?"

He shook his head and waved a hand dismissively. I went back to IDs. I shone the Maglite down at the card in my hand. Looked good. Something stopped me. I focused on the picture. Blonde girl. Nothing unusual. What took me out of my rhythm?

Then I read the name a second time.

Elizabeth Bathory de Ecsed.

I looked up. She'd dyed her hair with light purple streaks, the kind that would wash out by Monday, and was wearing a white tank-top with some pink slogan applied to look as though it had been spray-painted on. She wore some makeup, artfully and carefully applied. For all the world, she looked twenty-one. Had she gotten in Bob's line, she'd have already been inside partying.

"Hi, Countess," I said with a smile. "How's Bratislava this time of year?"

She'd been chatting with a friend in line with her and ignoring me up until that moment. Liza fixed her eyes on me in that dismissive, how dare this get in my way look so many teenagers have mastered. Then she registered who she was looking at.

"Fuck."

She turned and bolted.

My turn to curse, but I took off after her anyway.

"Be right back!" I yelled to Bob as I tore off after her.

Chapter 26

Liza made good time in heeled boots. Honestly, I was a little impressed. She was around the corner of the building and past the porta-johns by the time I started gaining on her.

Each step was a jolt of pain. I didn't stop to question why I was chasing her. If just *seeing* me made her want to run, I probably needed to find out what that was.

This side of the building, past the few folks milling around waiting for a bathroom, we didn't attract too much attention. I wasn't sure what her plan was, but I was confident I'd catch her.

And do what, hero? Spear-tackle a seventeen-year-old girl?

Luckily, that decision was made for me. The heel of her boot hit a hole and down she went, her bag spilling out of her hand and spreading its contents over the ground. I pulled to a stop and knelt down a couple of feet away.

"You okay, kid?"

"I have a name," she said, still defiant, despite a mouthful of grass.

"You okay, Liza?"

"Got a bad case of the indignities, but it'll pass."

I offered an arm to help her up. She waved it away and started to push to her feet. I decided to make myself useful and gather her bag. I turned my light in that direction.

And it shone directly on a bundle of needles held together with a rubber band, their tips still sheathed in orange plastic. I bent down and snatched them up.

Liza came up limping. I felt a tad bit less sympathetic as I held up the bundle of hypos.

"This looks like some pretty serious gear, kid," I said. "What're you doing with it?"

"I already said I have a name," she snapped.

"Yeah, and I'll start using it again as soon as you tell me what these are about," I said, waggling the bundle at her.

She limped over to me and made a feeble snatch at the needles. I held them out of her reach. She then held out an arm to me.

"Does it look like I use?" she sneered. "It's *Naloxone*, you ass. Because there'll be people here who *do* use, and someone's gotta watch out for them."

"So you're the party mom, huh? Not sure I'm buying that."

"Don't give a shit if you buy it or not. Gimme that back."

"Liza. The other guy at the door, my friend? He's a cop. Even if this is Naloxone and not narcotics, I don't think it's legal for you to have it. Pretty sure this is prescription stuff."

"So what're you gonna do now?" She stepped back, balled her hands at her sides. Still defiant. I liked Liza. I felt like a shit holding her over the frying pan like this.

"Were you ever Gabriel's party mom? Ever need these for him?"

She turned her head away, looked down at the ground. "No," she said in a very small voice. "But he's why I got them in the first place. I started to worry about him."

God. Dammit.

"Where'd you get the Naloxone? You can't just buy this shit at a pharmacy."

She looked up at me. Her eyes were getting wet in the corners, and it wasn't an act. I felt half an inch tall. She muttered something I couldn't hear.

"Where?"

She muttered again, but this time I heard it.

"Dr. Thalheim."

God. Dammit.

"Stay here," I said.

"Gimme my stuff back."

I turned and glared at her. "If I do that, you're gonna take off. Right?"

She shrugged.

"I'm not that stupid, Liza." I tucked the rubber-banded pack of needles into a back pocket and went back around to the front.

Quite a line had built up, and even Bob's wall-like equanimity was starting to flag as he dealt with it. I went to the door.

"Told you we weren't chasing people," he said as he scanned IDs.

"It…was relevant. To my job."

Bob looked up at me. In the shadows of his Maglite and the glare of the lights from inside the barn, I could see the lifted eyebrow and the question.

"Yeah. That job. I'll need a few."

He nodded. One thing I like about Bob Sanderson, if he puts me on to a job, it's because he trusts me to do it, and he doesn't try to look over my shoulder or manage me. He just lets me go. He knows I'll try to toe the line, but maybe also that there's parts of what I'll do that it's better he doesn't know about. Bob was as straight as any cop who'd ever existed. He could come upon three dead men in a hotel room with no next of kin and no way to identify them, each with a briefcase full of cash, pockets full of diamonds, and suitcases full of drugs, and every single item, to the penny, would go straight into evidence.

I stopped pondering silly hypotheticals and went back around the side of the building. I found Liza leaning against the side of the building, her shoulders heaving. She had the ankle she'd twisted stuck out awkwardly in front of her.

"Hey, kid."

"I told you I have a *name*. I mean goddamn, did it not bother *you* back in the dark ages when everybody called you champ or tiger or pal or probably 'big guy'?" She looked up at me, and there were still tears in her eyes.

"There you are," I said. "I don't know you all that well, Liza," I went on, emphasizing her name, "but you don't seem like a crier. So talk to me. You got the Naloxone from Thalheim?"

She nodded. "I haven't seen a friend die, yet. But the first time I came to one of these, last year, some kid I didn't know, just ODed right there on the dance floor. Everybody stood around like idiots, or ran, because they were afraid of it coming back on them if they did anything."

"What'd you do?"

"I ran. But not far. And then I called 911, and told them what happened and where to go."

"Good. And so you looked around for Naloxone. How'd you get them from Thalheim?"

Another sigh. But the tears had stopped. "Word around campus is he'll…do that sorta thing."

"What, provide medication?"

She nodded. "You know, nothing recreational. Not only recreational. But maybe Adderall. Maybe you get migraines, maybe you're afraid of watching your friends fall asleep and die."

"I get it. He likes to help." Maybe that's how she saw it. What I saw was a drug dealer in a position of power over children. With access to medically privileged information. I was also seeing a little darkness at the edge of my vision. But I didn't need to lay that on her just now.

"Yeah. So I asked him if he could get that."

"What'd he say?"

"He said it wouldn't take long. And he gave me one the next week. Said he admired the impulse."

"What'd they cost?"

She shrugged. "Pocket money."

"For you or for him?"

She snorted. "I don't think Dr. Thalheim is hurting for money. He drives a Porsche."

Of course he does.

She turned to me then. Once again, she was herself. Angry, maybe a little scared, but worried about her friend. I think the distance she'd shown me in her interview back in the school had been a defense mechanism, and I'd bought it.

This girl clearly cared deeply about her friends. Enough that she'd lie and spend money and risk herself and maybe commit a crime to try to save their lives. Or the lives of strangers, if it came down to it.

The teens will surprise you if you give them half a chance.

"Liza, I can't let you go in. And I'm guessing your friends already scattered."

"Probably."

"My friend the cop and I, we have to stay here till this shuts down. So I'm calling you a ride, and I'm putting you in it, and the driver's payment is going to be dependent on watching you go into a building where they judge you are safe. Okay?"

"Fine."

"If you'd like, I'll make sure to request a woman driver."

She was silent a minute. "Thanks."

I got out my phone and opened a ride-share app, input the appropriate info, using the address of one of the school's residence halls as given me by Liza.

"Are you gonna find Gabriel?" More worry coming through now. But not panic.

"Well, based on what you've told me, I just got a lot closer. You could've told me this on Tuesday."

"I didn't think he'd really be gone for more than a day, then. I thought he just…needed some space or some time. He feels pressure and it boils over."

"Pressure?"

"Running. Cross-country. Track. The coaches and recruiters are all over him and he hates it. He only does it because he's good at it, and feels like he needs it to pay for college."

"His dad could probably buy some colleges."

"Doesn't want his dad's money. Doesn't think his mom should have to pay after everything she's already done for him. So he's determined to get it himself and running seemed like the best way."

"I know a little bit about what that kind of pressure is like," I said. "When I find him, I'll try to talk with him about it. But I've got to find him."

"Are you going to tell anyone?"

"About you carrying these?" I took the pack of needles out of my pocket, kept one for myself, and handed her the rest.

"Why are you…"

"Giving you these back or keeping one?"

"Yeah."

"I need one to confront Thalheim with. Don't worry," I said, as I saw the panic rising in her eyes. "I'll keep your name out of it."

"But he'll know."

"I think he'll have bigger worries than who snitched, Liza. This could mean his license, his career, jail time."

"But that'll come back on me."

"I promise it won't." There my mouth went again, writing a check I didn't know if I could cover.

"How?"

"I can be very persuasive." I felt that black edge in my vision come back. My instant dislike of Dr. Thalheim was crystallizing now. I should've listened to my gut right away.

I was alerted by my phone that Liza's ride was here. "You need a hand walking there?" I gestured to the headlights that had just swept up the gravel road.

"Couldn't hurt."

I extended my arm, bent at the elbow, and she leaned on it. I walked her to the car, put her in it, and explained the situation to the driver, a slightly sleepy-eyed fortyish woman. She looked like a mom, probably driving for extra cash, in sweatpants and a t-shirt. The car was an older model Ford, a little loud, but scrupulously clean. My gut trusted her.

"You get your pay, and a fifty percent tip, when she's safely indoors and texts me proof of that fact. Okay?"

"For a fifty percent tip all the way to Furnace Bay, I'll carry her up the stairs to her dorm."

I eyed Liza, who was frantically shaking her head. She sat in the back of the car like the cheap upholstery might bite her. "I don't think we need to go that far." I gave the both of them one of my cards, and went back to the door.

The crowd had dispersed, since it had reached capacity. A few kids, without backup plans or just really desperate to get inside an old barn, milled around. Bob leaned against the front door.

"You get the first shift inside for leaving me in the lurch," he said.

"I'm sorry, man. I really am. That was important."

"The Kennelly kid?"

"Might be a break."

"Can you tell me about it?"

"Give me till Monday. I haven't gotten anywhere by then, I'll have something for you to follow up on."

"Fine. Get in there and watch the crowd."

Chapter 27

The rest of the night was generally awful. I gave dirty looks to any of the kids who seemed to even think about getting rowdy. I was agitated. I wanted to be working my case. Maybe kicking down Thalheim's door and redecorating his office by tossing him vigorously around it.

I was deep in a particularly violent visualization when Bob finally tapped me for his inside shift. Being back out in the night air calmed me down a little, and by the end of the night I had a rational plan of action.

I tried to give Bob a hundred bucks out of my envelope at the end of the night but he wouldn't have it. We didn't talk much on the way back to the marina. Bob could read that I was angry and also that I didn't much want to talk about the case, just work it. So we left it alone, listening to the crackle of his radio and the minor calls that came in around the county on a Friday night.

I didn't even have a cocktail that night. I both barely slept and slept well; I popped out of bed at seven a.m. without needing an alarm, got dressed, and started walking.

I was standing outside the firm's office when somebody came to open it up at 8:45.

"Matthew," I said, as my lunch partner of the other day eyed me strangely, keys in one hand, steaming travel mug in the other.

"You're not usually here early. Or on a Saturday. Or at all."

"We must be ever-vigilant and willing to do without the mortal pleasures of sleep and breakfast in the pursuit of our calling."

"What?"

"I got up extra early and walked here. Now open the damn door."

I barely waited for Matt to clear the doorway before I'd grabbed a set of keys and taken the same company car I'd driven earlier in the week. He yelled after me, something about paperwork and permission, but I didn't have time for that.

I drove straight to Farrington Academy, reasoning that a school with that big a boarder population had Saturday office hours, and likely enough nurses and guidance counselors on duty all weekend as well. Maybe I'd get lucky and Dr. Thalheim would be right there.

Without a suit I had fallen back on my rather small stock of collared shirts and unstained jeans. But it was a Saturday. Besides, the cut of this particular polo shirt emphasized my shoulders and my arms. Amy Riordan might be on the desk.

I knew the instant I buzzed that she was, because her voice sounded surprised. Perhaps even delighted.

"Mr Dixon!" The door buzzed and I swung it open, hopping eagerly up the steps to her office. I smiled, but it was a cold smile, for all that she looked lovely in a red half-sleeve sweater shirt, jeans, and matching red flats.

"Amy," I said, laying one hand on the edge of her desk. "I don't suppose Dr. Thalheim is in today."

She held up one long finger and flicked a few keys. "Looks like he's on call but not on campus. I can call him. He's got a private practice and consultancy in his home office." She was already reaching for the phone.

"Don't trouble yourself. Maybe just give me his number and I'll call him myself."

"Of course." She grabbed a Post-it and a pen and quickly wrote it out. "This is his practice number, and probably the one he's more likely to answer."

"Great." I brushed my fingers against hers as I took the note, smiled wider.

She blushed, but only a little. Fetchingly.

"You any closer to finding Gabe?"

Her use of the nickname gave me a moment's pause. Everyone else who knew him—his mother, Liza, even Gen as an employee of his dad—called him Gabriel. Maybe she wasn't as close to the pulse of the place as I had thought.

"I hope so. Just one or two things maybe Dr. Thalheim can clear up for me."

"Well I hope we'll be seeing him back here soon."

"Me too, Amy. Me too."

I won't deny that a part of me definitely wanted to ask if she might like to see me, soon, here or elsewhere. But I had blood in my eyes and the scent in my nose, and there was, as they say, no time for love.

Chapter 28

It took only a moment to find the address associated with Thalheim's private psychological practice. Or consultancy. Or surgery. I didn't much know or care about the term, just where it was. It was on a residential street not far off a golf course, one of the more well-to-do edges of the county. The kind of place a big paper would call a *leafy street* if big papers ever wrote about Cecil County.

I drove around the development. Broad lawns, big houses, two and even three-car garages. It looked new. I drove past a few For Sale signs. A quick glance at Zillow while I parked in a cul-de-sac revealed some eye-popping numbers.

Then again, I lived on a boat that only cost me the price of gas and marina space and labor, but that was only when Marty could catch me. How was I to know what was expensive or wasn't?

But it seemed to me that, driving a Porsche, owning a house that went nearly half a million, a twelve thousand-dollar watch, it didn't add up. I wasn't sure what Liza considered pocket money, but if her parents could pay the freight for Farrington, it was more than the three dollars and seventy-eight cents in my pockets at the moment.

I looked at the address. There was a sleek car shape, complete with spoiler, under a car cover, with the Porsche mark or badge or heraldry bright and yellow all over it.

"What an asshole," I muttered. The second time I drove past I heard the distinctive rumble of bikes. Loud bikes. I turned onto a cross street and pulled up to the curb, and they roared past behind me. Looked like standard suburban biker cosplay: leather cuts, shiny helmets, wallet chains, the works. It was Saturday morning, and a couple of guys who'd gotten tired of golf wanted to feel *bad*. I got a glimpse of the cut as they roared on; the patch on the back read *Aesir*, but I didn't get a good look at the design.

I pulled back around and parked in front of a house just across from Thalheim's. No sign of anyone stirring, not even to mow their lovingly tended lawns.

An addition on the side of Thalheim's house had a separate entrance, and light blocking curtains on all the windows. That had to be the practice. There was another car in the driveway, a standard SUV of some kind, this one with a sticker from some other local prep school on the back. I paused between that and the shrouded sports-car, doubting my approach for a moment.

If he had a receptionist, I'd have to make it on charm and bullshit. I could deal in both with the best of them, but I was running a little hot.

I could, if he was busy in the practice, quietly burgle his house in the pursuit of anything incriminating.

I looked to the front of the house. There was no camera, no shield-sticker in a window, no sign warning me off.

I wanted to. Boy did I want to. But I decided on the direct approach.

I sidled up to the practice entrance and tried the handle. It slid open. It led into a small sitting room, no one in it, just a row of IKEA chairs against the wall, a low coffee table with magazines spread on it, and a mini-fridge against the far wall. There was a door with a sign dangling from a nail by a cord that read "Session in Progress."

I glanced at my phone. It was 9:54, so I doubt I had long to wait. I glanced at the magazines: *Time, Sports Illustrated, Highlights*, the like. If I strained, I could hear the murmur of conversation in the other room, but that seemed intrusive. I picked up *Highlights* and flipped through it.

I was studying a page for the third or fourth time — really engaging with it — when I heard the conversation break up and a door open on the far side of the other room. Then the door facing me opened.

Thalheim was dressed in home-office casual. Neatly pressed khakis, tan loafers, a light purple shirt with simple silver stud cufflinks. He started to flip the sign when he suddenly registered my presence and did a double-take.

I saw a flutter of fear in his eyes, but he calmly attempted to resume control.

"Mr. Dixon. What are you doing at my home office? Any inquiries should go through the school."

"Really I'm just here for *Goofus and Gallant*, doc." I held up the page I'd been studying. "I'm wondering about a Utilitarian critique of the simple moral binaries of the strip. You know. What would Jeremy Bentham think? What if Goofus' actions lead to a larger sum of pleasure?"

He stared at me blankly.

"What, sharp philosophical dissections of legacy children's American pop culture not your thing, doc? It's just, I'm thinking of going back to school, and I'm looking for a thesis topic."

"What do you have to say to me that would require being in my home office?"

I set down the magazine and stood. I put my hands on the back of my hips as I walked till I was within just a foot or two of him. He smelled like too much cologne and a healthy dose of talc. His skin looked fake-tanned, but there was a trickle of sweat on his brow.

I pulled the capped hypodermic of Naloxone from my pocket and held it up.

"What? You use opiates, need some more of a drug you can't pronounce because you think it'll save you? You won't be able to use it on yourself."

I let him go on, just staring at him with the needle in hand. "Doc. I took this off a kid. A minor, who was trying to get into a party that had hired me to work the door. A pretty crazy break in my case, I know, but the kid told me they'd gotten it from *you*."

"That's nonsense. I don't distribute medication to minors without parental knowledge and consent, and *certainly* not something like that. A wild accusation."

"Is it, though?" I turned the needle around in my hand, tracing a bar code, some numbers. "Prescription drugs have *pretty significant* traceability, Doc. Would not be hard at all to find out what pharmacy this came from, who it was dispersed to, when, for how much, in what batch. Or at least, where it was *meant* to go."

That single bead of sweat became a trickle. He went a little pale under his tan.

"Bullshit," he sneered. "You wouldn't know how to find any of that out. They wouldn't release that information to some two-bit redneck hood pretending to be a detective."

"Just because I live in Cecil County doesn't make me a redneck. And where would that leave you? Anyway, my best friend's a physician's assistant who can find the information in moments."

"What do you want? Drugs? Cash?"

He'd gone from fear to anger to bribery and deal-making in record time. I decided to get more direct.

"Doc," I said, "what color would you call that shirt? Lilac, maybe?"

"What?"

"It's a nice color. The blood'll ruin it."

"Is that a th—"

He didn't get the words out. I didn't go for the face because I didn't actually want him bloodied. What I did do was drive a right hook straight into his stomach. He crumpled over the blow, turning whatever words he'd been about to say into a muffled *oomph*.

I grabbed the back of his collar with my left and dragged him through the open door into his office, dumped him onto the floor by sharply twisting him over my out-flung leg.

"I don't like hurting people, doctor," I said, a little shaking edge in my voice. "But now I *know* you sell drugs. To kids. To kids who are supposed to be in your care. So I'm having a little bit of a hard time thinking of you as *people*."

He had a little fight in him. He came up to his feet, heavy and slow, and looped a fist at me. I caught it, turned his wrist and ran his arm up behind his back. I duck-walked him over to his desk and pressed him face down against it.

"Gabriel Kennelly. You sell him anything?"

"No." His voice was muffled, with his cheek pressed against the wood of his desk.

I twisted his arm a little harder. "Are you absolutely certain about that?"

"I prescribed him drugs, yes, but those are on record."

"What kind?"

"That's privileged," he protested. Somehow he managed to sound aggrieved with his cheek mashed against the edge of his desk.

I could break his arm. I could twist his shoulder joint right out of the socket and leave him screaming in pain.

I hadn't been lying when I said I didn't like hurting people. I felt the band of a wristwatch on his hand and pulled his cuff up.

"This one cost twelve thousand dollars too, doc?" It wasn't the same one as earlier in the week. Instead of leather, this one was all gleaming stainless steel, or so I thought.

"It's a Breguet Type XXI," he said. "You could sell it for six or seven thousand easily. Take it. Take it and go."

"Doc, I'm not here for your watch or your money. I want you to answer the question I just asked, and if you don't, I'm going to pull this watch off your wrist and stomp it into splinters." He'd stopped fighting and gone limp against his desk. I pulled the watch free and threw it on the ground.

"What kind of medication did you prescribe for Gabriel Kennelly?"

"Pain pills. Anti-anxiety medication. I don't know the specifics of type or dosage. I'd have to check the school records."

"Why'd he need them?"

He shrugged. "Kids complain. Pain, stress, the usual."

"And isn't your job to treat them?" He didn't answer that. "You know anything about where he's gone? Ever heard of something called Ladders? Maybe it's a kind of rehab place?"

He raised his other hand in the air, started tapping it frantically against the side of his desk.

"Are you trying to tap out? This ain't a match, doc. This is me talking and you answering."

He made a kind of choking sound, and I suddenly realized I'd been leaning on him a little too hard. Sheepishly, I let him up, stepping back and away from him. He slumped to the ground, rotating his arm and massaging his shoulder. I stepped away and picked up the watch, letting it dangle from my hand.

Suddenly, he shot up and dove across his desk. He opened a drawer, frantically ruffling through it.

Thinking he was going for a weapon, I bolted around the other side of the desk, grabbed the back of his head, and bounced it sharply off the polished wood. There was a sharp *crunch* and he went limp, let out a sob, and brought his hands to his face. I opened the drawer and found a phone. I stuck it in a back pocket.

"You really gonna call the cops, doctor? That was your big play? Christ. You come up with a gun, that I could respect. But you're the drug dealer here. I'm just a righteous anti-drug crusader who got a little over-zealous. Who're the cops going to side with?"

He was still kneeling in front of his desk, holding his nose, crying around it. He didn't answer. I felt, perhaps, a smidgen of empathy. Not sympathy.

"Broken nose hurts like hell, every time. Or so they tell me… mine's pristine. But I can probably set it back in for you."

He fell back on his ass and scrambled away from me on the thick green carpeting. "Keep your hands off me, animal. I sometimes give Naloxone to the kids, sure. And maybe other therapies they need but can't get."

"Give? Because the kid I spoke to, they said they *bought* it."

He finally took his hands away from his face and looked up at me balefully. "I have to fund the purchase somehow. It's certainly no more than the families can afford. Most of them don't even miss it."

"I'm a little curious about how you make the drugs disappear, not gonna lie. But I'm here about one thing, and one thing only. Gabriel Kennelly. Ladders. Tell me what you know."

"Or what?"

"Or the next thing I do is let the Cecil County Sheriff's Department in on your little extracurricular chemistry club. And probably the state troopers, while I'm at it."

"You'll do that anyway."

"I might!" I smiled at him. "But telling me about Ladders is the only thing that could save you, so, let's have it."

He was no longer looking at me. His voice was quiet and resigned.

"It is a rehabilitation center," he said, very slowly and carefully. "I can get you an address."

"Good. Get it."

"It might take some time."

I dropped the watch to the ground theatrically, and lifted my boot over it. "Let's hurry it up."

He finally pulled himself up. His nose was floating; every step brought pain to his face and his eyes watered. "You don't want to do this."

"Do what?" I touched the heel of my boot to his watch, but I didn't crush it.

"Not the watch. This," he said, lowering his hands and trying to fix me with his watering eyes. "You don't want any part of it."

"I want one part. Gabriel Kennelly."

"It'll cost more than you're willing to pay."

"You've already got one broken bone today, Doc. Unless you're keen to add to that number, get me the address."

"I'll have to go into the house."

"How stupid do you think I am?" I pulled his phone out, set it down. Looking at it now, I realized it almost certainly wasn't his everyday phone. It was cheap blue plastic; it looked old and basic. Probably a burner. "Unlock the phone. Tell me the number you need to call. I'll dial it, and I'll hold the phone. You talk. I suspect for one second you're selling me upriver, you're trying to tell anyone anything, you're gonna eat the goddamned phone. You got me?"

"Not even a call. Just need to look it up. It's only on there."

He tapped open the phone. I held it flat on the surface of his desk and watched him open an email app. It moved slowly. I could read what he tapped in, just a quick search for "Ladders" in his email. I saw several pop up, and he swiped at one before I could read them all.

He looked up at me.

He held out the phone and I saw an address taking up the screen. It was in the county, off a state route, but nowhere I recognized. I stared at him.

"Write it down, asshole."

He snatched a fountain pen and a notepad in a thick leather portfolio from a table on the other side of the room, where there was a therapy couch and a chair, all in the same green leather as his office at Farrington.

He scribbled it down. I took it, carefully stuck it inside the fold of my wallet. He snatched at the phone, but I smacked it out of his hand.

"Paperclip," I said.

"Why?"

I cracked my knuckles.

He got me a paperclip and I popped open the little compartment of his phone with the SIM card and dumped it into my hand. That, I also carefully slipped into my wallet.

"You can have that back when I find Gabriel. Understand something, Doc," I said as I stood from where I'd been sitting on the corner of his desk. He scurried away from me. "If you're any deeper in this thing...drugs, kids using, selling, putting them in rehab to bilk insurance money...best you just tell me now. If I have to find out, I'm gonna come back here, and I won't be as agreeable and placid as I have been this morning."

"If I ever see you again, you'll regret it," he sneered.

"Way I see it, Thalheim, you call the police, you have to explain everything I came to talk to you about. Even if they come grab me, I just tell them what I know. They start talking to kids at Farrington. Whatever story you give them blows up. I've got you by the balls. I'm not letting go that easy."

"I didn't say anything about cops," he said, and his voice had a new kind of confidence in it. I shrugged.

"I'm not all that worried about the state licensing board, either."

I turned to go and then I had a stray thought. I walked back to him. He'd picked himself up and summoned his dignity, standing up straight and adjusting his shirt-cuffs, then bending to pick up the watch.

I grabbed the hand with the watch and held it up. He jerked it away, pulling it protectively against his chest.

"Where's the other one?"

"The other what?"

"The watch you were wearing the other day."

"Why, do you want *that* one?"

"I don't want any watch. Just curious." I took a picture of it with my phone and sent it to Brock, with a single word and a question mark: Retail?

"It's in the winder in my study," he sneered. "I don't expect you to know what that is."

"I can read the context clues," I muttered, as I turned to leave. I looked back at him. "Remember, Dr. Thalheim. I've got you by the balls. It can't feel great, but don't do anything rash. If I don't find Gabriel Kennelly, I'm coming back. And I'll have the license plate number of that sexy little German number in the driveway ready to send to my friends at the sheriff's."

"You'll regret this," he said from the door of his office.

"Probably," I said with vague wave as I went out into the driveway.

I did snap a pic of that license plate on my way out. Then I got in my company car and set my GPS for the address he'd given me.

On my way out of the development I heard the rumble of bikes again.

Chapter 29

I did set out for the coordinates I had, way up in the woods near the state line with Pennsylvania. But I had to pull over after a few minutes of driving.

My hands had started shaking. I steadied them by placing them in my lap after putting the car in park on the side of the road. I took a few deep breaths.

"Just adrenaline," I said aloud, to no one else. "Just all worked up for a fight and he wasn't much of one." My body was reminding me that what I'd said to the doctor about hurting people had been true. I thought about how easily I could've broken his arm. I could hear the snap of broken bone. I gave my head a shake.

I felt a chill, and then suddenly sweaty. My stomach roiled. I was glad I hadn't eaten anything.

I turned on the car's AC, said aloud, very carefully, "He sold drugs to kids who came to him for help."

That seemed to calm it, me, the body that I suddenly didn't have much control of, down. I put the car back into gear and eased onto the road. It was a solid half hour from where I was now.

I drove robotically, thinking only of finding the kid. The kid who might be a drug addict, or at least a user, whose friend was worried enough about him to start buying Naloxone off their school psychiatrist.

"Which means she knew to do it, and other kids know it. If other kids know it, faculty know it. How does that kind of rot spread?"

I put that out of my head, because Google Maps told me I was close. It was a residential area, but the kind where every house had an acre or so of land around it.

I pulled up across from my destination. Tall privacy fence around the back. Heavy drapes in the windows. No lights on that I could see.

"Well," I said aloud. "It's bright goddamn daylight on a Saturday, I have no backup, no weapon, and nobody knows where I am."

I decided to doublecheck the no weapon part. I killed the engine, took the keys, and opened the car's lockbox under the passenger seat.

No gun, thank Christ. No Taser. No spray.

But there was a novelty paperweight of the kind sold in any number of shops along Route 40 between New Castle and Baltimore. Which is to say a heavy piece of metal with a handle and sturdy, even pointed, loops around the knuckles. I slid my fist into it.

A little tight, but it would do. I felt better.

With my hands in my pockets I walked straight up to the door of the building. No signage, but there was a small, cheap-looking camera pointed right at the front door. I couldn't see any lights on it but I did keep my head down.

"I gotta start wearing a cap," I muttered.

I tried the door and it slid open at the slightest push.

Inside it was a goddamn ghost town.

I felt anger well up in me, and I wanted to rush into the place and start tearing it apart. I stood in place and counted, slowly, to ten, with my eyes closed. Then I tried to do it in Latin. Then Greek. I didn't get past four in either one.

It was a pretty standard three-story home. I didn't know what kind of style. The kind where you walked into the living room. There was a large TV against the wall to my left and a ring of chairs near it. Beyond that I could see the kitchen. A set of stairs rose up on the other side, and in the kitchen it looked like there was a basement door.

First, I went and touched the back of my hand to each of the chairs in front of the TV. Two were warm. Then I went into the kitchen.

Dishes were piled in the sink, cheap plastic stuff, with plastic silverware that looked like it was designed for children. All color-matched. I grabbed a towel from where it sat on the counter and immediately regretted it when I felt an accumulation of sticky grit on it. But I used it to open the fridge anyway.

Lots of packaged and processed stuff, water bottles, individual juice boxes. Individually wrapped cheese slices, a huge stack of industrial lunchmeat.

The fridge was dirty. I wouldn't be surprised to find roaches in the folds of the part that sealed the door.

I gave up on the kitchen and went upstairs. There were three bedrooms. One had a queen mattress and box spring on the floor, shoved in a corner, with sheets strewn all over it. The other two had single mattresses laying on the floor, with cheap blankets and cheap, uncovered pillows on them.

Heavy metal bars had been mounted on the walls of that bedroom, on all sides. I went and tested them, pulling on them with my hand wrapped in the towel.

If I laid down and braced my feet against the wall, I could yank them clear. I had no doubt. But if I was shackled to one? If I was an addict, or in a haze from being medicated?

They were at just the right height to shackle an ankle or wrist and keep someone from slipping away in the night.

A bathroom with a glass-walled shower. None of it had been washed and all of it reeked. I forged in anyway, wishing for a clean towel to cover my mouth with. The mat in front of the shower was still wet. Hair lined the sink and the drain in the shower.

With the towel still wrapped around my hand, I pulled open the linen closet. Plain white shelves stacked with junk.

Including an industrial quantity of Ioperamide, both Immodium and the generic variety. Box after box of it. Ladders had been providing "services" and "therapies" alright. The absolute bottom tier of both, but for top shelf prices. Gen had redacted most of what was on the claims statements she'd turned over, but the charges for Ladders had been long enough to put four or five digits before the decimal.

I turned on my phone's flashlight, and reminded myself, not for the last time, that I should bring my damn Maglite on investigations and not just door jobs. I squatted down—wincing as my ribs rebelled—and peered into the closet.

There was a clear handprint in the back, where no boxes of anti-diarrhea medicine—or in this case, poor man's Methadone—were stacked.

A section of wall slid open. Inside it were two marble notebooks, the kind I remembered from middle school. Piles of receipts. And two plastic zipper bags full of much smaller bags, each containing white and beige pills. I popped open one of the notebooks. It was indecipherable, giant block-like letters that I couldn't make any sense out of. Definitely not English. Perhaps a kind of code.

I took all the paperwork, stuffed the receipts inside one of the notebooks. I left the drugs.

"Should probably get out," I muttered. But there was still a basement. And the cord from the camera mounted by the door ran down to it.

Down in it I found a bare concrete floor, a circle of chairs, some IV racks with nothing on them. A chest freezer. I almost dreaded opening it, but it was full of labeled sample jars—though there was a numbering system I couldn't read.

The other side was full of cheap frozen food. Pizzas, hot pockets, chicken nuggets, and popsicles.

There were two windows high up on the wall, facing the neglected lawn. Below them was a simple folding table with a power strip connected to an extension cord. Several component cords were scattered around, as if they'd been left behind when a computer had been quickly disconnected. I looked carefully over the table. There were silver candy bar wrappers and empty Utz bags scattered around the table and the folding chair that sat in front of it. But there was definitely an undisturbed rectangle in the middle where a computer had sat.

"Took the computer, disconnected the security camera," I said, glancing up the wall, where the cord of the cheap camera had been sloppily secured to the wall with painter's tape. "But forgot to go upstairs and get the secret shit."

My hand curled into a fist inside the towel and I wanted to bring it down in the middle of the table. I was furious. Thalheim had played me — sent me here when he knew he could scatter them somehow. Which meant there was another location out there.

But I was closer, and I had threads to pull.

I texted the address to Bob, along with a quick message. "Oh no. Help. Please come to this address immediately. Signed, P. Rob Ablecawz."

Just because I was angry didn't mean I couldn't take the time to poke fun at Bob. I hustled out of the place, folding up the towel and sticking it in my back pocket — after wiping the doorknob with it — and sauntered casually back to my car.

I felt my phone buzz. I ignored it and drove.

Chapter 30

I debated driving home to the marina and the *Belle* or heading back to Thalheim's. There's no way he'd have stayed put, so I thought I better be a little oblique about approaching him. Plus, my ribs were throbbing and I wanted at least some Advil. It was almost 11 a.m. Sun would be over the yardarm soon.

I settled on home. My phone buzzed a couple more times as I drove, but I wasn't going to flagrantly ignore the rules about handheld phone use and driving. Not when I'd just burgled a house-slash-shady rehab clinic and had a passenger seat full of evidence I'd stolen.

I was not eager to test the limits of the Cecil County Sheriff's patience with my particular brand of derring-do.

The drive passed easily, mostly with me hoping to find a list of addresses or patients in the notebooks I'd taken. But they had proved a mystery when I glanced at them at stoplights, the letters in them looking more like they were etched with a pen held in the fist rather than written.

"Might be time just to go to the cops," I wondered aloud as I turned into the marina.

I stuffed the notebooks into the glove box of the car, and headed for my dock.

Then I stopped and turned back to the parking lot. There was a bike in it. A big, shiny, chrome-and-gray bike. American, long exhaust, loud. It seemed out of place.

There's certainly crossover between bike owners and boat owners. All the same, I didn't often see folks come out to the marina *on* their bikes. People came to their boats with coolers, PFDs, sunscreen, picnic baskets, cases of beer, fishing tackle, camping gear, luggage, folding bicycles. Or they came towing their boats just to use the launch, if they weren't renting a slip and didn't feel like driving to a free launch.

But you didn't do either of those things on a motorcycle. Sure, it could've been a friend of a renter. Could've been a lot of things.

But I'd noticed it, and I didn't notice things for no reason, in general.

I started walking more carefully, more gingerly. I gathered myself and then tried to tune all my senses to the air around me, to every sound, every breath of air, every single sight that might be out of place. Most of the people who were taking their boats out for the weekend were long gone by now. The parking lot had been largely empty, which is probably why I'd noticed the bike.

And when I turned down the dock, with my slip at the far end of it, I saw the *Belle* shifting back and forth. More than she would've with the river lapping at her.

I dropped into a crouch and started taking careful, quiet steps.

Once I got to the edge I could hear somebody moving around. On my boat. In my *home*. They were in my bunk. I heard a drawer open and shut.

"Well," I breathed, "fuck everything about that."

I took my shoes off. With exaggerated care, I slipped over the gunwale and padded softly onto the deck by the stern. I looked down the main passageway.

There was a stocky, not very tall fellow, rummaging through my possessions and generally making a mess of my galley. I heard the clink of a bottle.

I snuck down the passageway. He was so absorbed in his task, muttering to himself, that my clumsy stealth was every bit good enough. He was wearing jeans, a sleeveless black t-shirt, and a leather cut that said "Aesir MC" on a patch over a bird's skull design in the middle.

He also had a knife lying along his right hip. This would be a tad tricky.

I could probably get the knife out of his sheath and smack him around with the pommel end. I could certainly have tied him up and bashed his face repeatedly against a flat surface. But I didn't want blood on my deck, or on my hands.

I decided on a direct approach that, if I did it right, would take him out quickly and relatively painlessly. I slipped up behind him, threw my left arm around his neck, grabbed my left fist with my right hand, and squeezed.

His arm flailed for his knife, but I felt him go limp before he could do anything to grab it. Down he went.

I had no time to clean up the mess he'd made. I grabbed some rope from the chain locker—really just a small cooler I had tied in place along the stern rail, between the benches. I quickly bound his hands and feet. I took the knife—an odd thing, sharp along one side, with an angled blade and some kind of horn handle—and set it on my chopping block. I clambered up the ladder to the wheelhouse and started the engine. Then I went back to the railing and slipped the lines free.

I got back at the wheel and puttered slowly out into the river.

Chapter 31

By the time my guest awoke, we were well out of sight of the marina. I knew a little cove that was just out of the major boating channels and surrounded on three sides by what looked like thick forest. In reality, if he concentrated, he might be able to hear the rumble of passing trucks. We weren't all that far away from civilization.

It just felt like we were.

I had dragged him out onto the deck behind the main cabin and tied his hands to the gunwale. Then I'd pulled out a folding chair and sat, legs crossed, waiting for him to join me. I studied his knife while I waited.

He didn't wake up quickly, nor did he adjust well to his surroundings. He tried to sit upright, found he couldn't, then started struggling against the ropes.

"The Boy Scouts taught me knots," I muttered. "The Navy made damn sure I remembered them. So I'd give it a rest. It's good rope. You're not getting out of it."

He opened his mouth and let out a wordless bellow. Birds startled into the air from the nearby banks. I sighed, stood up, set his knife down on the chair. With cupped hands, I boxed both his ears. Not as hard as I could. Not by a long way. Hard enough to get his attention, sure, but not to damage his hearing or burst an ear open.

He shut up, his eyes screwing up against the pain.

"You do that again," I said, "and I'll do it with my fists instead of my open hand. You got me?"

His face still contorted with the pain—nobody could really deal all that well with getting their ears boxed when they were helpless to do anything about it—he spat at me.

"You have no idea what you're up against, you fucking amateur," he growled.

"I think I have an idea," I said, lifting the knife. "I think you're some kind of biker cosplayer. Why you're on my boat, though…that I don't know. What were you doing?"

"I don't have to tell you shit."

"Whatever it was, I'm betting it wasn't particularly legal. So I don't think you're going to call the cops."

"Not telling you shit."

"A variation on the theme." I stood up and started rummaging through his pockets. My hands closed on a zip bag and I pulled it free. It was full of small white and beige pills. Not unlike what I'd seen at the house I'd just tossed. There was also a card with the address of the marina and *Belle of Joppa* written on it.

"You here to plant drugs?" I held up the bag and shook it at him. "This seems like a lot just for one little guy to get through the day. This is probably enough to get you charged with intent to distribute."

He started pursing his lips as if he were going to spit at me. I raised a clenched fist and lurched toward him.

He quickly thought better of it. His spitting face turned into a defiant sneer.

"The use of narcotics is forbidden among the Aesir. We must keep our bodies as pure as our Nordic blood."

"Sweet, merciful Christ," I muttered. Bikers and racists. Real winners.

Then aloud I asked, "You a strong swimmer?"

"What?"

"Like, strong enough you think you could get to the bank with your hands and feet tied up? Because the fewer questions you answer, the less likely I am to cut any of your bonds before I kick you off my boat." I was bluffing; I wasn't about to chuck him overboard and let him drown. He didn't know that.

He paled, a little. But there was still defiance in him. I tried a different tack.

"Why does your cut say 'Thrall' on it?"

"Because that is my role until I earn my way into the band."

"The band?"

He looked a little sheepish. "The club."

"Ah. So it's what you call a prospect. Aesir, huh? Like Norse gods?"

"The old gods are the only gods that matter. All others are weak. All others pale before the might of Odin, and Thor and *ow*."

I cut him off by cracking him atop his head with the butt of his knife. I didn't have time for the Viking wannabe spiel that, added to being a one-percenter gang and racists, made them a real idiot trifecta.

"Answer my questions, or learn to swim like a goddamn eel. Who sent you?"

"My Jarl," he sneered.

"You have played too much *Skyrim*."

"You wouldn't understand."

"I think I do. Thrall is a prospect. Jarl is, what, a club president? Some kind of officer." I started tapping the knife against the flat of one hand. "Who told him to send you?"

"Thralls do not question. Thralls take orders."

"But you were sent here to plant drugs? And then, probably, call the cops to tell them about the drugs. How'm I doing?"

Silence again, but with less starch in his expression than before.

"You know Doctor Thalheim?"

His eyes widened and he tried to sit up straighter.

I smiled. "You do. So he called you. I even saw a couple of your pals around his development today, didn't I? What the hell do you chucklefucks have to do with a guy like Thalheim?"

"Once Aesir, always Aesir," he muttered. "Oaths are for life. Not the whims of a man."

"Doc used to be a biker, huh? Shit. I can almost respect that." I tapped the knife a few more times, mostly because I could see it agitated him.

"What's the matter," I said, making sure to get my fingerprints all over the blade. "Worried about tarnish and rust?"

"I cannot go back to the hall without my seax," he admitted haltingly.

"That's this, huh?" I set it on my lap. "What's the arrangement? You supply Thalheim with drugs? He sell for you?"

"I don't know," he said finally. "I know the Jarl speaks with him. I know he identifies...sales targets. That's as much as I know." He had broken now, looked like he was pleading. "I've only been in a few months." Behind his patchy dark beard I could tell he couldn't have been much more than eighteen. Maybe not more at all.

"If I let you go," I said, "can you set up a meeting?"

He shook his head. "I'm just a thrall. I'm new. I'm nobody."

"What's your name?"

He hung his head. "Thralls don't have names. Thralls obey orders."

I needed to get this sad idiot off my boat before I started feeling sorry for him.

"Listen up. I'm going to cut you loose from the rail. I'm going to help you stand up. I'm going to cut the bonds on your hands and feet. Then I'm kicking you right off the boat. You try anything, I'll turn your lights off again, and *then* I'll shove you off the boat."

"How'd you do that?" he suddenly asked. "Sleeper holds don't work that fast."

"Not a sleeper hold. A choke hold—blood choke, not air choke. Ischemic response."

He looked at me like I'd just spoken Russian. "Ischemic response. Drop the blood pressure to the brain too far too fast, and the lights go out. Don't make me do it again."

He nodded reluctantly. I cut free the rope tying him to the rail, then helped him to his feet. He stood a little stooped.

"If I come back without my seax, they'll punish me."

"You'll have to risk it." I pushed him up against the stern railing and cut his feet loose. Then his hands, and I gave him no time to adjust. I did exactly as I told him. I literally kicked him off my boat.

He was too startled to do much more than splash around and yell. I let him flounder for a bit, then said, "Put your feet down. And walk the opposite way from this boat. I'd hate to see you get chewed up by the screw."

"What about my seax?"

I held it up so he could see it. The early afternoon sunlight reflected off the blade.

Then I turned and hucked it over the central tower of the boat, as far into the river channel as I could manage. It hit with a loud *plop*, and instantly sank.

Then, ignoring his yells, I clambered back up to the wheel and started the engine again.

Chapter 32

I couldn't see that there was any percentage in going back to my usual dock, so I set a course for a restaurant with a marina attached.

On the one hand, this MC knew my usual address. If I didn't have business I could just stay out on the water but that wasn't an option. As I made my way out into the Susquehanna and up toward Port Deposit, I thought of my plan of action.

I picked up my cell and dialed my boss.

"Jack, if you're calling me at home on a Saturday it better be because you found the kid and a chest of fucking diamonds."

"Look. I'm close on those. But something's gone sideways."

"You owe me dinner, then."

I was taken aback. "I…what?"

"I told you this was a tricky case. You said it'd be open and shut. We bet dinner on it."

"Fine. But right now, I need two folks to go over to the marina and pick up the car I left there."

"Why two?"

"Because I still need the car." I filled him in with most of the details. I elided the MC, just alluding to them as muscle that Thalheim apparently had access to.

"Wait. You're sitting on a drug-dealing school psychiatrist, and an insurance fraud, and you haven't called the cops in on this yet?"

"I want to find the kid first," I said. "He gets swept up in that, with drugs in him, who knows what happens to him."

"If he gets arrested, you still get paid for the hours you've worked, and his whereabouts will no longer be in doubt."

"Jason," I said, "give me till Monday to find the kid and extricate him from this mess."

"You sure you can do it that fast?"

"Yeah." I was lying. It was okay to lie to the boss; everyone knows that.

"Fine. You pulling up to the Landing?"

"Yep."

"All right. Someone'll be along presently."

I had a nice long think as I made my way to the restaurant. Jason was right; I needed to turn this over to the cops. But nothing good was going to come of Gabriel getting arrested. Or anyone else.

Once at the Landing I tied up and waved off the somewhat cautious approach of the waitstaff. I saw a manager that I knew and told him to bill the firm. Then I paced in the parking lot.

Chapter 33

About a half hour later, the company Nissan pulled in to the restaurant parking lot. Brock unfolded himself from the front seat of the Nissan and waved me in.

"Uh, shouldn't there be another car here to drive you back to the office?"

Brock shook his granite-slab head. "Nope."

"Brock, I don't…"

"I know, but the boss says you roll with backup today. No ifs, ors, ands…" He paused as he stumbled over the cliché.

"Fine, but I'm driving." I waved him away from the driver side and slid into the seat. He pulled in next to me.

"Boss had another rule, too."

He handed me a locked black plastic case and then handed over the key.

"Goddammit." I unlocked it. The foam held two holstered weapons. The larger was the yellow and blue Taser. The smaller was matte black.

"Goddammit," I repeated. "Is this also not optional?"

"He says if you don't carry it, I'm supposed to text him. And then he'll call it all in."

"Goddammit," I said with increasing anger.

"Take it up with him, man."

"Fine." I closed the case and handed it back to him. "We've got a doctor to see."

* * *

It was a quick drive and I didn't fool around this time. Thalheim's Porsche was still in the driveway, uncovered.

But there were also two bikes parked behind it, and one on the street.

"Shit. All right. Give me that case."

I put the Taser on my right hip, nice and visible. The pistol was a Beretta Storm SubCompact.

"Christ," I said, as he put it on the back of my belt and pulled my shirt down over it. "I hope I don't have to shoot at anything. Won't be able to get my finger inside the damn trigger guard."

"Actually Beretta rounds the guards in order to…" Brock got a look at my face and shut up.

We started across the street. I wiped my palms on my thighs. I went straight for the front door rather than the office, and it opened in our faces.

Two bikers filed out and flanked the door. Both had the same kind of cut the idiot on my boat had had, only theirs read "Huscarl" on the left breast. They looked a little more together than the thrall I'd kicked into the river. They had the same kind of knives on their belts, and long beards—one red, one dark blond like mine—braided with silver decorations. Ravens, Thor's Hammers, and wolf's heads seemed to be the design motif of choice.

"Enter," one of them said. "Speak with the Jarl."

"Ooh," I breathed. "Is he going to send me to hunt down a dragon? Clear out a nest of bandits? Will this count toward Becoming Thane of his Hold or…"

"Enough with the jokes," the redhead said, dropping his hand to his knife. "Now give up your weapons."

"Nope. Not going in there unarmed," I said.

A stronger, more confident voice came from inside the front room of the house. The lights were off and the sun outside was bright, so I couldn't really see inside particularly well.

"Let them in. We have our blades. In close quarters, their firearms will do the cowards no good."

I hear that a lot. All things considered, if it did come to a tussle, and I had to choose a gun or a knife, even at close quarters I'd take the gun. Most handguns have plenty of sharp and hard surfaces on it that work for striking. The pistol whip is a classic for a reason.

But you can't shoot anyone with a knife.

We walked in. The door closed behind us, with the Huscarls clomping in after us on their engineer's boots.

The front entrance faced a stairwell and led to a kind of fancy sitting or living room on the left, and a dining room with a long table on the right. We went to the right. Thalheim stood against the far wall, behind the table. In front of him, seated, was a man considerably taller than me or Brock, given the way his long frame loomed over the end of the table. He had black hair, a strand or two of gray in it, worn in a long lock, with the sides of his head shaved.

He didn't seem to be built too big—not with my shoulders or Brock's arms. But those tall bastards could fool you. If it came to a fight, I wouldn't want to have to deal with his reach. And there was something unnerving about him.

It might have been the eye patch, thick dark leather embossed with the same bird's skull motif as on the back of the cuts, that covered his left eye.

But he was also completely and utterly still. His hands lay spread on the table, silver raven and wolf and runic shield rings gleaming in the soft interior light. His one eye, bright blue, focused tightly on us, watching our movements.

"Should we sit?"

"Only if you want to." His voice was as big as he was.

"Okay, then. I'll stand." I put my back on the wall and rested my hands on my hips. Brock took the hint and went to the opposite wall.

"I'm really only here to talk to Dr. Thalheim," I said, pointing one finger at him. His body language didn't make him seem any happier to be here than I was. Arms wrapped around his chest. Chin low. One ankle crossed over the other. He wouldn't meet my eyes.

"Instead you will talk to me."

"What do I call you? And what about?"

"Call me Jarl Troy. And about the fact that you have interfered in Aesir business. I presume you think you have a good reason to have done so."

"Looking for a lost kid."

"So I hear. Not a kid, though, is he? Old enough to make legally binding decisions."

"Old enough and smart enough are two different things."

He smiled, very faintly. It was the kind of smile that did not make his eyes move. "This is true. You have some measure of wisdom, but how much? That you are here, and I have not heard from him, means that my Thrall failed."

"Well, his phone probably got fried when I kicked him into the river," I said with a shrug.

"How was he taken?"

"Unawares," I said. We stared at each other while I refused to elaborate. Something leather creaked. There was a lot of it in the room.

"I suppose you see yourself as the hero of the piece. Is that so, Mr. Dixon?"

"It's not a piece. It's a kid's life. And it could still mean something. To him, his mom, his friends."

"What is it to you?"

"I looked his mother in the eyes and told her I would do everything I could to find her son. I'm doing it."

"For pay, of course."

"Gotta eat," I said with a shrug.

"And if you locate the boy, what do you plan to do? Immediately involve the authorities?"

"I just want Gabriel Kennelly. Free and clear."

Jarl Troy stared at me. I'd been stared at by drill instructors, angry master chiefs, hungry sailors, and disappointed wrestling coaches as long as I could remember. I stared back.

"This particular part of our venture is perhaps as profitable as it was going to be," Troy said. "We will arrange an exchange. Peter. Give Mr. Dixon pen and paper."

Thalheim produced a pen and a pad of paper from his shirt pocket and walked over, handing it to me. His eyes fixed mine.

There was already writing on the first note, in very small handwriting.

633 Harvest Ridge

I took the pad and pen and looked at Troy as Thalheim stepped away. "Where's the meet? Conditions?"

He named a nearby shopping center. I wrote it down and snatched that first Post-it off the pad, stuck it in my pocket. On the fresh page, I wrote my cell number and handed the works back to Thalheim.

It must've galled him, acting as some asshole's errand boy inside his own house. But I could see a visible relief in his eyes when I'd swiped the top page.

"Leave now. Wait for our call." Then he looked to his two Huscarls, both of which tried the hard stare on me as we left. "See, Carls? That is how business can be done between plain-dealing men."

We headed back to the car. I resisted the urge to dig the Post-it out of my pocket immediately. I started up and drove out of the development, then immediately pulled over.

"You drive," I said as I pulled the paper out and plugged 633 Harvest Ridge into the GPS app.

"Why? They haven't even set up the meet yet."

"We're not going to the meet, Brock. Drive like you fucking mean it."

The little four-cylinder engine roared as Brock put it into gear.

Chapter 34

As soon as Brock got us on the road I pulled out my phone and dialed Bob.

I didn't wait for a greeting when he picked up. "It's your old friend P. Rob again. Meet me at—"

"I'm not on retainer, Jack."

"I think I've got it this time. Him. The kid."

"Well, I'm still tying up the first place you sent me to. Jesus, Jack, what was going on here?"

"I think you get a first-hand look if you meet me where I just told you to meet me." I felt myself slammed against the door of the car as Brock took a turn on what had to be two wheels. Three at the most. "But you need to do it silent. You come in wailing, or with a big caravan, and it's all going to shit."

"You got any more preconditions?"

"Yeah," I said. "Unless the kid is literally doing a felony the first time you clap eyes on him, you let me take him out of there. If I'm right, there's a whole host of bigger shit for you to shovel, don't worry."

"Fine. I'll be on my way as soon as I can get someone to take over here."

We hung up. I began to worry about the possibility of encountering any of the state or county's finest between here and the house, but either luck was with us, or Brock just drove too damned fast for any of them to spot. It was possible the car blurred out of sight as he drove.

"Why'd you call a cop? Didn't you just tell the biker you weren't gonna?"

Brock glanced at me as he drove. I slowly turned to fix him with an incredulous stare.

"I lied to him, Brock."

"But if you get a reputation as a liar…"

"I don't give a shit what a bunch of biker criminals who've played too much *Skyrim* think about me, Brock. Who the fuck are they, anyway? You ever heard of the Aesir MC?"

He shrugged. "Just didn't think that was how…you know."

"You've read too many novels."

"I don't really read much. Except *Men's Fitness*." I held up a hand to stop him. We'd gotten deeper into the forest primeval with every turn the GPS had sent us on, and now we were on Harvest Ridge Road. Every third house looked like it had fallen down, or was in the process of falling down.

"I know most of this county is in the middle of the damn woods," I said, "but this feels particularly middle-y and woods-y."

"Always heard this wasn't a great neighborhood. Used to make shine out here, they said. Then they said they were making meth."

He pulled up outside 633, which was a single story over a basement, clapboard walls, dilapidated tile roof, screens falling out of the windows sort of place.

"Wait," Brock said, as I spilled out of the car, checked my weapons, and started for the front door. "Shouldn't we make a plan?"

"Yeah," I said. "The plan is follow me."

I got up a head of steam and lowered my shoulder. I was too angry and too focused to think about how much it might hurt, but the shock of pain down my ribs reminded me.

Whatever. I'd worry about that later. The door bowed inward and splintered when I hit it.

The interior of the place smelled like piss. There were a few huddled shapes on the floor to my left. In a kitchen on the right, someone bulky in scrubs was busy sorting things on a Formica counter.

Of more immediate concern was the man in the leather cut whirling around to face me, eyes wide. He was whipcord thin, and none too fast on his feet, with a long wispy beard bound in iron rings conveniently within reach. I grabbed it and yanked as hard as I could, introducing his face to my knee. He stumbled backwards, scrambling for his knife, but I was on him. I pinned his knife hand with my left, squeezing the wrist as hard as I could, and I hit him once, twice, three times in the side of the head. The first two were warm-ups. The third was as hard as I could, with form, twisting my hips into it despite my back screaming at me.

His eyes went distant and he stumbled against the counter, dropping his knife from a hand that suddenly wouldn't obey him. He would've crumpled if I hadn't been helping him up. My back and my ribs shrieked in painful protest, but the adrenaline was beginning to drown them out.

The heavy person in the scrubs in the kitchen started shrieking. He was a man, I could tell that now. I let the biker drop to the floor. He hit it with a gurgle, then tried to reach for his knife. I stepped on the side of his knee, sharply, and he let out a groan and lay still. I bent down and picked up the knife.

I pointed the knife at the guy in the scrubs, meaningfully. "Shut. Up."

He backed away, though there wasn't far for him to go in the tiny kitchen, putting his hands up. I saw meds on the counter, carefully apportioned in three piles.

"Gabriel. Kennelly," I said. He pointed behind me.

"Brock," I said. "Watch them. If the biker or the nurse moves, do something terrible." I unholstered the Taser and held it out to him. He took it, sweeping his hands to cover both his targets. He looked a little ridiculous, but he seemed focused on the task, at least.

I went to the blanket-covered heaps on the ground. The way they lay made me think they'd been drugged. I pulled the blankets loose.

The first thing I noticed was that all three had their hands zip-tied.

The second was that the one in the middle was Gabriel.

Chapter 35

I used the knife I'd taken off the biker to cut them all loose, and chafed their arms and cheeks to get them awake. I managed to get them into chairs, at least. The tiny house had an old battered sofa and a couple of folding chairs. The other two looked Gabriel's age, or younger. One girl and one boy.

"Jack," Brock said. "Our biker pal is waking up."

"Encourage him to stillness," I said.

"What?"

"Kick him a couple of times." Some thumps and a groan followed, indicating that my erstwhile partner had taken my advice.

"Gabriel." I knelt in front of the kid, having sat him on the couch. I gave some gentle slaps at his face. He woke up enough to look at me, his eyes fluttering.

"You, in the scrubs," I shouted. "Get your ass over here."

"If I move he's gonna tase me!"

I stood up and threw him a glare. "If you're not walking over here by the time I finish this sentence, I will come get you. You do not want me to do that."

His shoes squeaked across the floor as he hurried to my side.

"What are they on?"

"Nothing much," he said. "I just had to give 'em a bigger dose than usual to get them moved. Mostly methadone."

"Mostly?" I grabbed a handful of the back of his scrub shirt and yanked, forcing him to look at me.

"They'll be fine," he said, "I swear. Nobody's gonna OD. See, look," he said, pointing to where Gabriel had lifted his head and was speaking. "He's coming around now."

It was true. Gabriel lifted his head and focused his eyes on us. He didn't have pinned pupils or any other signs I knew of.

"What…who're you? Where are we?"

"Gabriel," I said. "My name is Jack. Your mom hired me to find you. I'm going to call her and tell her to come get you, okay?"

He nodded, then let his head thump back on to the couch. I pulled out my phone and dialed her number.

"Mr. Dixon?" She answered on the first ring, breathless, worried.

"I've got your son here with me, Ms. Kennelly," I said.

"Where is here?"

"I want to caution you that he's alive, but he may need medical attention. Not in the vein of immediate intervention but on a more medium-term basis."

"I don't care. I'll deal with that as I have to. Where is he?"

I gave her the address. She hung up.

The guy in scrubs had started to edge away, so I grabbed him again, and I pointed to his three patients.

"They all better be fine to walk out of here, you got me? Anything happens to them…"

Meanwhile, a phone started buzzing in the biker's pocket.

I let go of my grip on the would-be nurse, and took the phone from the other biker's pocket. It wasn't an area code I recognized. I shrugged and answered it with a simple "Hello."

"That is not the proper greeting for your Jarl, Anthony."

"Anthony's unable to answer his phone right now."

"Mr. Dixon." The voice was somehow muffled and amplified.

Bluetooth inside a helmet as he rode? It seemed likely. "You disappoint me."

"You sound just like my dad."

"We had a deal, Mr. Dixon."

"No. I had a job, and I did it."

"Have you gone so far as to involve the authorities?"

I looked to the front door. No sign of Bob. "Nope."

"Well. Then you may yet be allowed to live. But there will be repercussions. We were planning to abandon this particular venture regardless. But perhaps not as quickly as this."

"You like hearin' yourself talk, huh?"

"Do not involve the police in our affairs, Mr. Dixon. That would be a grievous error on your part."

The door swung open, and was suddenly full of a somewhat angry-looking sheriff's deputy.

"Go catch an arrow in the knee," I said before ending the call. I dropped the phone on the biker's back and went to Bob.

"Tell him to put that weapon down," Bob said, pointing at Brock. I waved at him and he lowered the Taser. "Now. Explain."

"I will," I said, "as soon as I get Gabriel to his mother."

Bob looked over at the three patients. He pointed at the guy in scrubs. "Are you their nurse?"

"Yeah. Yeah. I'm the nurse. I take good care…"

"This can't possibly be up to any kind of…code or standard or whatever facilities are supposed to have. You're under arrest." He lifted the back of his polo shirt and pulled a pair of cuffs free. I raised a hand.

"You might want to save those for him," I said, pointing to the still unmoving biker.

Bob looked at him, went over and grabbed his wrists, cuffing them quick. He ran through the usual stuff, though I wasn't sure the biker could hear him.

The nurse looked at the door hungrily.

"I wouldn't," I said. "I'm not a sprinter, but I'm sure I can catch you. And I'll be angry when I do."

Bob yanked the biker on to his feet with an assist from Brock. "I'm taking this guy to the truck. Coming back with zip ties."

Chapter 36

By the time Bob had the nurse—whose name was Nick—zip-tied, arrested, and stored in the back of his truck, I managed to get Gabriel moving around. The other two had also woken up but didn't show too many signs of being talkative. I'd gotten names: Lisa and Hayden, but not a whole lot else, and that had taken some real work.

I figured I still had a few minutes, so I got out my phone and made a call.

"Jack," Dani said, "if this is about anything other than scheduling a training session—which you badly need, by the way—or coming over to our house to make the Beef Wellington you owe us—I don't want to hear it."

"Good to talk to you, too, oldest and closest of friends."

"Fine. What?"

"I just need a referral. Not necessarily an official one, just... if I've got some people who might be dopesick, need treatment, real treatment, not the ER, not a fly by night rehab place, do you know where?"

"Take them to the ER if you have to, for a night or two, because no addiction treatment doc is gonna see them on a Sunday afternoon. But I can have some names for you by tomorrow. Is that it?"

"That's it."

"When do we get our steak doughnuts?"

"You wound the grand tradition of English cookery with that glib reduction, madam."

"You're Scots and Irish, Jack, and you've never before said 'grand tradition of English cookery' with a straight face."

"Wednesday. Provided I don't get arrested." I glanced at Bob as I said that. He waved me toward the door with an annoyed face. I gave him a thumbs up.

"Is that a possibility?"

"Eh, so long as I keep my mouth shut I'm fine. See you Wednesday. Four?"

"I want to eat before eight."

"Better make it three, then." I hung up, gathered Gabriel, and went outside to wait for his mother.

"These all the clothes you've got?" He blinked against the sudden glare of bright September afternoon daylight. He was wearing a sweat-stained white t-shirt, too-large green sweats, and stretched-out gym socks.

"I guess," he said, his words slow and thick, clearly through a dry mouth.

"How much do you remember of the last week?"

"Not…all that much," he admitted.

It was about then that his mom pulled up.

She didn't even turn off the engine of her car. Just ran to him and threw her arms around him. Despite the five or six inches in height he had on her, she just about lifted him off the ground.

"Ms. Kennelly," I said, coming close and speaking just to her. "You may need to get Gabriel some medical attention. You may need to dance around how he got into the state he is in. Do you need help with that?"

"My sister's a nurse," she said. "Can I take him to her first?"

"Well, she'd know better than I would. Long drive?"

She shook her head.

"Go," I said. "Do what you've got to do."

"When will we, you know, settle?"

I waved a hand. "This week sometime, if you can manage it. Don't worry about it right now."

She gave me a wave and bundled her son into the car and pulled away.

Bob walked up next to me. "Aesir MC? Guy's cut just calls him… Huss-carl," he said.

"Huscarl." I corrected the pronunciation. "And…some kinda Nordic racial purity thing going on with them. Ever heard of him?"

"Can't say I have. But I can do some digging around, if you think they're gonna be a problem."

I shrugged. "Let's go over this whole deal first. You're going to want to go pick up a Dr. Thalheim."

Chapter 37

The rest of that afternoon and evening was spent endlessly recounting my investigation. First, to Bob, then to other members of the sheriff's department at a station, then to a state cop in plain clothes. She didn't look happy to be there or to be talking to me. At every stop, I elided any mention of Liza, simply telling them that I'd picked up on a "rumor" that a member of the school's counseling staff had been willing to supply drugs to the students of Farrington.

"And how'd you know it was him?"

"Well," I said, "he was the only one wearing a twelve-thousand dollar watch and driving a ninety-thousand-dollar car. He sorta stood out."

The cop had looked at me over her reading glasses then. "Consulting psychiatrists can make a lot of money."

"Sure," I said. "Especially when they're selling drugs on the side."

She frowned at me then, but nothing much sterner than that.

"You've picked him up and he's started blabbing, right?"

The frown became a full-on disapproving stare.

"For what it's worth," I said, "he gave me the address of the place where you found those kids. And he did it at a risk to his own well-being."

"How's that?"

"He slipped it to me while the Aesir MC was stomping around his house and ordering him around like a lackey."

When I said Aesir MC she flipped through her legal pad. "You ever heard of this Aesir MC before? Know anything about them?"

"Only what I gathered from their symbols, dress sense, and nomenclature."

"And what's that?"

I shrugged. "Neo-pagan, but the kind that gives the rest of them a headache and a bad name. Most of 'em are just folks, but these guys have a racial purity hard-on for Odin and Thor and Freyja."

She stifled a laugh. "Meaning what?"

"They're assholes?"

"What else?"

"Well, they used archaic terms. Thrall for prospect, Huscarl for full-patch, Jarl for chapter president, I think. I didn't exactly see the organizational flowchart."

She jotted a few notes with her fountain pen. "Look, you hear from these guys again, you remember anything they said, maybe you give me a call." She took a card from a pocket and handed it to me.

It had her name and rank: Detective Sergeant Janine Dominguez. I slipped it into my wallet. "They a big club?"

"Don't know. Haven't dealt with them much in Maryland. Bigger presence in Pennsylvania."

"Seemed like a pack of poseurs and cosplayers to me."

"Well," she said with a professional smile, "you serve on a few organized or gang-crime taskforces and maybe I'll care about your opinion, Mr. Dixon."

I felt a little stirring of the hair on the back of my neck, but I wrote it off. Jarl Troy had seemed a little frightening, but surely he had bigger fish to fry than a PI who blew up a scheme he admitted wasn't working.

Finally, well into the evening, they cut me loose. Brock had long since disappeared, so Bob drove me back to the restaurant/marina in Port Deposit.

I went silent and waited for him to talk. It took a few minutes.

"You didn't do too bad with this one, Jack," he finally said.

"Don't go burdening me with compliments now, Bob."

"You found the kid, I'll give you that. And in pretty short order. And you probably only committed a couple felonies along the way."

"Everything was exactly where I found it. Anybody with injuries fell. Except me," I said. "In case you've forgotten, I've got facial contusions and back spasms. Possibly broken ribs."

"Dr. Thalheim made some noise about unlawful entry but he shut up about it pretty quick. I'm not real sure of the legality of you busting open the door of the second address. But there was some real shit going on in there. I don't see how the county or state is going to want to prosecute you for any of it."

I was silent throughout. My capacity to deal with cops—even cops I liked, and I certainly liked Bob—was wearing thin. "Hooray," I said weakly.

"As for this Aesir MC, I did a little reading of some internal files." Bob steered a while. "Nothing I can share with you, but these guys seem like pretty bad news. You might want to keep your eyes out."

"I'll sail into the middle of the Chesapeake," I said. "And wait until they develop an amphibious motorcycle."

"You got to come to shore sometime. And we're not that far off from winter. You got a place to stay?"

"I'll figure something out." We were silent but for the steady drone of the SUV, the crackle of the radio. "I, uh, I've got some evidence you're going to want. Notebooks, ledgers, maybe? Written in some kind of code. Runes, I think, now that I know what I know about the club. And receipts. I took them from the first house."

"Where are they now?"

"Probably at the firm. Brock's got as much imagination as a sled-dog, but that means he'll also take absolutely anything I left in the company car and lock it up inside the firm."

"You probably shoulda told this to the state cops."

"Leaves you with the big collar. Makes you look good. Least I can do, given that you put me on this job."

"Well," Bob said, "I knew if there was something to latch on to, you'd be the one to do it."

"I'm touched."

"Don't be. If it had gone on much longer, it would've become my problem."

"Ahh, you can try to distract and divert, but I know what you meant. It was a compliment to my investigative prowess and perseverance. I know it. You know it. The world knows it."

"Before you go congratulating yourself, Jack, I don't think you're hearing me about the MC."

By then we'd reached the parking lot of the restaurant, which was jam-packed. Bob idled behind a few parked cars. I sat up a little straighter.

"They're mostly out of eastern, southern, and central PA," he went on. "And they don't really screw around. They drop bodies, and local law enforcement seem to have a hard time making cases stick."

"Well," I said, "since they all carry knives, and I have a permit to carry a weapon with currency in this century, I'll let them worry."

"There are members of the MC called 'Utlagr,' or some shit like that," Bob said. "And *they* carry the guns. Best I can tell, those members operate entirely outside the rules the rest of the MC has to follow."

"Huh." I was too tired and too hungry to really work myself up into a lather about this. "This sounds like something I can worry about tomorrow."

"And the day after, and the day after. But I can't convince you to take your life more seriously than you do." He hit the button that unlocked the door.

"Thanks for the ride."

"I'll want all that paperwork tomorrow."

"Yup."

I walked through the restaurant and went straight to the bar. I found a bartender I knew, ordered two pints of Guinness and the largest cheeseburger on their menu, in a box. With the vegetable of the day instead of fries, because I didn't deserve quite that much joy.

I finished both pints by the time the box came. I took it to the *Belle* with a couple more cans of Guinness the bartender slipped me. Then I crawled into my bunk, set an alarm for nine a.m., and drifted off to sleep with the muted sounds of late-night diners drifting over the water of the Susquehanna.

Chapter 38

I was slow to wake up the next day. The alarm music was Steve Earle today, and it took till the second verse of "Mercenary Song" for my brain to grasp it was time to get up.

"Well they say a man's got to do what he's best at, ain't found nothin' better so far..."

I let the rest of the song play as I stood, stretched, and immediately shouted in pain.

"Goddamn," I said aloud, putting a hand to my tender ribs. "I might have to get that prescription filled after all." I made my bunk, rooted in the fridge for the good peanut butter, savored all three tablespoons of it I could eat.

My phone had two missed calls and a voicemail, but I elected to ignore all of that, hit the gym, do some grocery shopping, and head into the office at my leisure.

I was briefly confused when I went outside and saw the stacked chairs and empty tables of the restaurant's deck.

"Huh."

Then I remembered I wasn't at my regular marina, and that a walk to Waterfront Fitness was probably more of a cardio workout in and of itself than it would typically be. And I hate cardio.

I made the executive decision to punt working out till later in the afternoon, after I figured out what I could and couldn't do with my current injuries. Then I got myself a ride and headed to a grocery store.

Grocery shopping was easy. A half-gallon of milk, as many jars of expensive high-protein/low sugar peanut butter and almond butter as my wallet could stand, a bag of carrots, another of apples. Shopping for Wellington ingredients could wait until after I got paid, I decided, after checking my bank balance. That led to putting back one nine-dollar jar of coconut almond butter.

I was checking out and waiting for another ride when my phone rang again. It was a work number. I almost flicked it away, but decided to answer. Three calls in one morning was a little much.

"Good morning, boss," I began brightly. "Calling to congratulate me on a job well done, no doubt."

"Jack." There was an edge in Jason's voice. A couple of hairs went up on the back of my neck. "Where the *fuck* are you?"

"The grocery store?"

"Get to the office. Now."

Luckily I already had a ride arranged. I just had to change the destination.

Chapter 39

When I shuffled into the office carrying my grocery bags, the place had a pall over it. People were gathered in knots talking in hushed tones. A few turned to stare at me.

I set the bags down on a nearby chair. "What?"

Jason stalked out of the management hallway and waved me to his office. He shut the door behind him carefully.

"Where the hell have you been?"

"Sleeping off an adventure like a hobbit, and then grocery shopping."

"Brock got shot last night."

Silence reigned. I could hear his wristwatch ticking. My heart thudded loudly; I was surprised he couldn't hear it.

"What?"

"He was ambushed and shot on his way back to the office in the company car. He's at Union."

"How is he?"

Jason shrugged a little. "He'll live but he's hurt. He got shot, for Christ's sake."

"He talking?"

"Pretty doped up. Not making a lot of sense."

"Notebooks," I said. "I'd taken notebooks from one of the rehab houses. Were they in the car?"

Jason raised an eyebrow at me. "What do you think?"

"God. Dammit."

"Those should've been turned over to the cops right away."

"I know. I just…"

"Wanted to go sit on your boat and drink whiskey and meditate on your brilliance by yourself," Jason said. That he wasn't shouting — that he was, instead, speaking in a quiet and clipped way — indicated how angry he really was. "You were lazy. And your partner got shot for it."

I immediately wanted to protest the use of the word partner but wisely thought better of it. If nothing else, he'd been my responsibility. So had the notebooks.

"How do I make this right?"

Jason's nostrils flared at me. "There are loose ends to tie up. Make sure the cops have everything they need. Make sure the client has everything she needs. Then go see Brock at the hospital."

"I'm gonna do the last one first."

"No, you're not. Corporal Sanderson and Detective Sergeant Dominguez are on their way over. You're gonna go over this stuff top to bottom with them."

"And do myself for B&E?"

"Oh please, you had reason to believe people were in distress in the house." He waved a hand vaguely. "Trooper'll have bigger fish to fry on the narcotics side and you set up a pretty nice high-profile bust for her. Bob's not going to grab you for penny-ante shit like this. Just be up front with them."

"Fine. Let me go make a list." I turned for the door.

"Stop. Sit right here." He tossed a pen and a pad at me and pointed to a chair in front of his desk. "Make your list. If you walk out that door I know you're gonna make a run for it, and I've had enough of that shit from you for a while."

Privately I admitted that he was almost certainly right, so I did as he said. I wasn't happy about it, but it sure seemed like my continued employment depended on it. I started the list.

1. Cops.

2. Talk to Ms. Kennelly.

3. Talk to the school?

4. Talk to the dad?

4b. Call Gen.

It was starting to look unlikely that I'd make my date of Wednesday to make Dani and Emily dinner, but I had enough threats hanging over me at the moment. While I was writing my list, though, the seed of a plan started to form in my mind.

It was about then that Detective-Sergeant Dominguez knocked on the door and she and Bob ushered me into a conference room.

Chapter 40

"**A**re you willing to go to jail over the identity of the student or students who told you Doctor Thalheim was selling drugs?"

"How many times are you going to circle back to that, Sergeant?"

"As many times as it takes before you realize I'm serious," she said, leaning forward over the desk. We'd been in the conference room for an hour by that point, and I'd laid out everything except Liza's name.

And one other thing, but they didn't seem willing to ask about it.

I looked with pleading eyes at Bob, who sat silent, with his arms folded over his chest.

"I'm not giving up a kid's name unless that kid specifically tells me they are willing to speak with you."

"We can compel that."

"You can try," I said. "Throw me inside if you want. I like spending time by myself, lifting weights, and reading."

"I meant the kids."

"Oh," I said, now leaning across the table myself to go eye to eye with her. "And how's that going to work? Uniforms all over a boarding school full of the richest kids in three states? How are the parents going to feel about that? How many of those parents make big donations to the Police Athletic League and the Policeman's Ball and to the campaigns of the legislators who make your budgets?"

I could see I had her then. She sat back and turned to look at Bob, who shrugged.

"I have a preexisting relationship with the school," I said. "Let me go in, talk to the administration, maybe some of the kids, and see what they are *willing* to do without making a big production out of it."

"Because you've been so good at avoiding that so far," Dominguez said.

"Look, I've handed you something pretty big. And I think Thalheim would cooperate if you lean on him."

"If his lawyer doesn't have everything thrown out because you muscled him and broke into his house."

Hmm. That changed the calculus a little, but only a little. "Do you have to have kids to make the case?"

Dominguez and Bob glanced at one another. "No," Bob finally said. "I doubt it. He has made indications he wants to cooperate. But we'll sleep better if we do."

"So we're still on the same page as before. I'll go to jail rather than give you a kid's name. But I will go to the school and see what they want."

"And do what," Dominguez said, "collect a consulting fee from their parents?"

"No," I said.

"We're not paying you."

I sighed. "I don't expect to be paid to go to the school. I need to do it anyway as part of my wrap-up."

The detective-sergeant raised an eyebrow. "Really?"

"Really."

"And who do you need to talk to there?"

"Do you really think I'm that stupid? I'll go to the school and talk to who I need to talk to, and if any of them are willing to talk with you, I'll let you know."

"Just trying to figure out your angle," Dominguez said.

"His angle is that he already fucked up on this thing once, and he wants to make sure he finishes the rest of it," Bob said. "Neatly."

"That's part of it," I said, nodding in agreement. "And the sooner you let me go, the sooner that process can start."

"Fine," Dominguez agreed. "Go on. But I want to hear something by Friday."

I left the conference room and went to gather up my groceries. I lingered outside the door to try and talk to Bob on his way out. He shot me a glare.

"Should've given me the damn notebooks right away," he muttered on his way out the door.

I didn't really have a response to that, so I just let him walk out.

I took a set of company keys and made my way to the hospital.

Chapter 41

When I got there, visiting hours had been suspended and I could do nothing but sit on my hands for an hour or two. I ate an apple and cracked open the first jar of peanut butter from my new stash. It was a heck of a lot tastier than the protein-added stuff. I decided now was as good a time as any to knock another point off my to-do list and call Ms. Kennelly.

She answered on the first ring. "Mr. Dixon. Once again, thank you."

"No need, Ms. Kennelly. I need to find out if there's anything else you need from me or the firm. And if you want to schedule an exit interview before we close out the case and move on to the minor details."

"Like billing?"

"Yes, like billing, but that's not really what I'm calling about. Is there any kind of help Gabriel needs that I can point him to? Anything else I can do?"

"Well, that depends on if you know anything about…" She paused and I knew what she wanted to say and what she meant, and also why she did not want to say it.

"I have a friend getting me a list of doctors. Board-certified in addiction medicine. I'll pass it on to you as soon as I have it."

"I don't suppose you had any luck getting in touch with his father."

"I haven't, no."

She sighed. "Perhaps I can call him. He may want to speak with you. Perhaps offer some kind of reward."

"The fee you pay the firm will be plenty. I'm not looking for a reward."

"Do you know…I mean have you reconstructed what happened?"

"I don't have all the facts, but I can speculate. As long as you understand that what I say is speculation and not necessarily correct."

"That's fine."

I took a deep breath. "Gabriel got into some drugs. I don't know what kind, but probably opiates of some kind. Not sure what else, or from who, to start. Dr. Thalheim had ties to criminals and he apparently helped identify kids for them to sell drugs to. Recently, they began moving from simple drug sales to insurance fraud. Dr. Thalheim was their point man on that, as well." I decided not to mention the MC, since I didn't want to do a bunch of explaining, or put rumors out there that might help scuttle the investigation that had no doubt started.

"What…what is the point of whisking a child away into rehab?"

I decided not to argue over the legal definition of child in this case. "It can be quite lucrative if the individual has good insurance. And, frankly, it was an employee of your husband's company that sent me working this angle. The rehab had started billing that insurance about a week before Gabriel's disappearance. From what I saw, the charges could have easily totaled tens of thousands of dollars in fairly short order."

"And what kind of services were they providing?"

"Very poor, ma'am," I said, trying not to think too hard about the metal racks bolted into the wall in the first house I'd busted into, or the zip ties lying around.

"Well," Ms. Kennelly said, "thank whoever that employee was. Take them to dinner. I'll throw in a tip so you can do just that."

I felt a little guilty smiling given my surroundings, and the reason I was there. But I did. "I think that's advice I will definitely take, ma'am." I paused. "Do you have any idea what Gabriel would like to do next?"

"He's going back to school. If Farrington will take him."

"I'm going to be visiting the school tomorrow, if you'd like me to make any inquiries in that regard."

"What time can I meet you there?"

"How does ten a.m. sound?"

"Perfect."

"Thank you, Mr. Dixon."

"You can call me Jack, ma'am."

"Susan, then."

"Tomorrow at ten, then, Susan."

Chapter 42

I waited out the closed hours scrolling the news and checking email. When visiting time resumed, I entered the intensive care unit, looking for the room number I'd gotten at administration.

The TV was on, flicking channels. That was a good sign. Brock was sitting more or less upright in his bed, TV remote in hand. He had a couple of lines in, and he had a bit of a glassy-eyed look.

"Hey, kid," I said, leaning against the doorway.

Brock's eyes drifted slowly over at me. "Jack," he drawled. "How are *you*?" I laughed a little.

"Question is how are you, Brock."

"I got shot," he said, with the bleary-eyed enthusiasm of the heavily medicated.

"Yeah, so I heard. You remember what happened?"

"Motorcycle pulled in front of me, cut me off," he said, swallowing hard. "Another one pulled up alongside and started firing into the car."

"What'd you do?"

"I popped out the driver side door and returned fire. I don't know if I clipped any of them. Definitely hit a bike, 'cause I saw sparks. Maybe got one with a ricochet. But they got me in the shoulder. The shooter dove into the car, rummaged around, then they drove off."

"That was my fault, Brock. They were after their notebooks, their paperwork. I shoulda given that to the cops. Never should've been your responsibility."

He waved his left hand — the one with the remote — dismissively. His right arm was immobilized in heavy bandages and a sling. "Eh. I got shot. Will have scars. Chicks dig scars."

If he hadn't been doped up with a bullet in him, I might have taken the moment to deliver some talk about demeaning and infantilizing terms for women, but he didn't seem likely to absorb anything just now.

"You gonna be alright? Back in fighting trim soon?"

"Month or two, I guess?"

"How's your insurance situation?"

"I...don't really know."

I nodded. "I'll talk to the firm about it, help you get it straightened out if need be." I looked around. "You need anything? Food, some reading material? Anything from home?"

"Man, if I could get some music somehow? They won't let me turn my phone on in here."

"I'll hit Wal-Mart and grab you something portable, with headphones. If you give me your passwords I can probably load your music library onto one."

I stood around awkwardly for a minute while he flicked the TV. "Orioles play at four," I said. "Getaway game before their last road trip. Might be worth turning on."

"Eh, I don't really watch baseball, man." He let out a jaw-cracking yawn and awkwardness resumed.

"Brock. I'm sorry," I said, looking down at my feet. "I shouldn't have put you in this position. I should've stayed with you, and I never should've left that evidence with you. This is on me, so anything I can do to make it right, you just tell me what it is."

I heard a faint wheeze, looked up. Brock's head had fallen back on his pillow, his eyes had closed, and he was drooling freely onto his chin.

No machines were making any unusual pinging noises or alarms, so I assumed that was just restful sleep.

A nurse tapped me on the shoulder and pointed toward the exit. I knew better than to argue, so off I went.

Chapter 43

At long last I got my groceries home, thankful that the milk had at least been refrigerated while in the office. I peeled a carrot with a paring knife and let the peels drop off the stern. I didn't quite have a carrot down like I did a potato; I couldn't get the entire peel off in one go. But I was getting closer. I'd only needed to reset the knife once.

Man's got to have goals.

I chewed on the carrot meditatively. It wasn't good. They never were, without butter or salt or at least a little balsamic glaze. But the Navy had taught me to strictly avoid scurvy, and I usually only had citrus in cocktails. I didn't much feel like drinking.

Which wasn't entirely true. I definitely felt like I wanted a drink, but I didn't exactly feel as though I had *earned* one. So I kept the bar closed.

I did get a card out of my wallet and dial a number.

On the third ring, a warm, slightly throaty voice answered. "Hello?"

"Gen. It's Jack Dixon. From last week."

"Oh, I remember you. Have you made any progress?"

"In point of fact, that's why I'm calling. I located Gabriel yesterday, and he is…recovering at home."

"Well, that's good news. I'm glad to hear it."

"And, to give credit where credit is due, your tip about Ladders proved fruitful. Helped break the case."

"That's good. Is Gabriel okay?"

"I believe that he will be, though I can't say too much about it. I am, however, under strict orders from Ms. Kennelly to thank the person who provided the fruitful tip. And so, I was wondering if you might be willing to accept a dinner invitation. As a thank you."

"I think I might. Where at?"

"Hrm. You know Skipjack, in Newark?"

"Heard of it, haven't been."

"They do great seafood, some of the only acceptable crab cakes over the Maryland state line, if you ask me."

"When?"

"Saturday? Sevenish?"

"Sounds like a date. I'll meet you there?"

"Perfect," I said.

"Then I'll see you Saturday."

"Great."

"Yep."

Another awkward silence. She laughed into the phone. Not quite a giggle, not a chortle, I wasn't sure what to call it. But I liked the sound of it.

"Goodbye then."

"Bye!" She hung up. I sat with the phone in my lap. The day was looking up, a little. I reminded myself that a young guy I was supposed to be watching out for had been shot by an outlaw MC obsessed with Vikings that was still roaming around. I'd had a plan percolating in my mind for that, if it became necessary.

I decided it probably was.

Chapter 44

So the next thing I did was call my drug dealer.

Really, Eddie is just your typical salt-of-the-earth weed farmer. He has the greenest thumb in the county. I have no doubt that if he wanted to grow heritage strains of corn or award-winning roses, he'd do that. Instead, he grows the finest all natural, organic, medicinal, and recreational herbs known to man. Or at least to me.

He is, as any man in his position would be, a tad paranoid. While Maryland was moving in the right direction medically, he wasn't too interested in joining a closely regulated — or at all regulated — marketplace. And it wasn't just about legal repercussions. Eddie was genuinely worried that someone would steal his secrets or force him to cut back on the purity of his experiments.

So when calling him, one had to be circumspect.

Eddie only took new customers by referral, and you'd get a certain set of hours and days when you could call him. Luckily, mine were on.

As always, he answered in dead silence. I couldn't even hear him breathe.

"Eddie. My favorite man of the soil."

"Jack."

"Hoping to talk to you."

He paused. Probably checking the handwritten schedule he kept and then destroyed every week. "Tonight. Or Thursday."

"Tonight, I guess."

"Eight p.m. The trailer. Do not bring your phone."

"How am I supposed to find it, then?" Eddie moved his camper here and there, hauling it on the back of a farm use truck.

"Write down the directions. Like an adult."

Eddie was, it needed to be said, a tad fussy, and a bit old-fashioned.

"Fine. Give them to me."

Eddie proceeded to dictate a set of directions that included at least two unpaved roads and a left turn into a field, followed by another left turn at a lightning-struck tree. I dutifully copied them all down. I still had a few hours before his proposed meeting time, so I did the only sensible thing, and went to the gym.

* * *

Early tests indicated that my ribs and back were going to be an impediment to most of the basic parts of my workout routine. Squatting was out. Deadlifting was out. Cleans and jerks and the bench press and all its variations were out. I was pretty good at disregarding pain, if I say so myself. But I had proven to myself so many times that I'd disregard it until I hurt myself really badly that I'd finally learned to listen.

So I puttered around the dumbbells for a while, doing a quick complex of as many different curls as I could think of. Front, back, switch, extensions, careful lunges, overhead presses that didn't hurt too badly so long as I kept my trunk incredibly calm. Still, it took far too long to work up anything resembling the good sweat a more robust lifting program would've generated.

And when that was done, I slunk off in defeat to the cardio area, and stared at an exercise bike for a solid two minutes before shame won out, and I climbed on.

At least I had a tablet, so I could get some reading done.

A little over an hour later, I stumbled out shamed and defeated, but at least I'd been at the gym, and no one had tried to talk to me. Traffic zipped by along 40. I was getting far too used to a car and I sat in the driver's seat resentfully for a full five minutes before I could bring myself to start it. I eased into the light afternoon traffic. Trucks and SUVs and old beater cars whipped around me. Life in Cecil County went on like it usually did.

I kept two ears open for the rumble of bikes. I didn't hear any, but that didn't make me feel a whole lot better.

* * *

The drive to Eddie's trailer was uneventful, but I was there a couple of minutes early. Rather than sit in the car and drive him crazy, I got out and walked up to the door. It was a retro-looking Airstream but, I suspected, was of more modern construction. The gleaming aluminum sides looked pristine and it seemed destined for beautiful western skyline camping. Frankly, it seemed more than a little out of place parked just outside the woods here in Maryland, with a smell of brackish water in the air. It was a wonder he kept that thing looking as good as he did.

Eddie's truck, a nondescript red Dodge pickup, the kind you might see thirty of in a day driving around here, was parked nearby.

I knocked on the door, only just resisting the urge to make it "Shave and a haircut."

"You're early," came a voice from within the shell.

"I like to give myself a lot of lead time, just in case."

"You're early," he said. "You can wait until the time of our appointment."

"Eddie," I said, "are you really going to make me stand out here for two minutes?

There was no answer. An amount of time that I guessed was probably exactly two minutes passed, and the trailer door slid open.

I walked in. The trailer was sweltering. Eddie didn't seem to mind. He was the kind of skinny guy who was so intensely focused on whatever he was doing that he probably never noticed the heat, the cold, that he was hungry, or tired. I'm not sure he would've noticed if he caught on fire. He wore a black t-shirt, jeans, standard work boots, and an Orioles cap featuring the ornithologically correct bird that was so old and stained it had all but turned blue, and black-frame glasses. He was older than me, but how old I wasn't sure.

"What are you looking for?" Eddie had two slide-open coolers at his feet. He slid down the lid of one. "I have some amazing butter if you're looking for something edible. Made with Blue Lightning. I know you look to relax, maybe take the edge off all the punishment you give yourself."

"Whoa, whoa. Let's pause the too-close-to-home psychoanalysis for a minute, and also ignore the implication that I'd ever *cook* with your product."

"You don't cook with it, you *infuse* things with it," Eddie protested.

"Well, what am I gonna do, inject all the candy I don't eat with it? You know I'm a traditionalist. But...I'm actually not here to buy. Not yet. Still haven't gotten paid from my latest case."

"If you aren't here to buy, then what are you possibly doing?" Eddie slid his cooler closed and stared at me, hard. Not in a threatening way, just in the way he looked at whatever single thing he happened to be paying attention to at the moment. Eddie did one thing at a time, just one, and he did it intently. His glasses were fogging up from the heat inside the trailer and I don't think he noticed.

I noticed. Sweat was breaking out between my shoulder blades, on the small of my back. I told myself it was the heat in the trailer.

"I have some compelling reasons to seek out contacts with someone who moves harder stuff. And more of it. Not," I quickly added, "to get into the business. To maybe deliver them a friendly warning."

"I don't get involved in the politics, the factions, the turf," Eddie said sharply. "I just want to tend my plants. I barely even make a profit. I pour everything back into the soil and the processes."

"Yeah, Eddie, I know. I get it. All I'm asking, as a loyal customer who'll be coming back to see you as soon as he's got the money to make a purchase, is for a number to call. A way to reach out."

"And why would I know that?"

"Because you operate with impunity, so someone is leaving you alone. And you have access to distribution networks. You can't be all on your own."

"You'd be surprised. I don't like to let my crops out of my hands, because you never know what someone else will do with it."

"I notice you didn't address my first point."

He looked away. "I do know a number. I can give it to you. But you have got to leave me out of it."

"Absolutely."

"Why do you want this, all of a sudden?"

I shook my head. "Better you don't know."

Eddie sat down heavily. The trailer was sparsely furnished. A small deal table, with some bags and gloves and tools on it. Two chairs. I didn't try to take the other one.

"This cannot come back on me, Jack," he said, eyes fixed on the toes of his boots.

My gym shower was now a total loss, sweat starting to soak my shirt. I wanted to get this over with and get back out into the cool night air, get back to the *Belle* and drop anchor somewhere offshore. But Eddie needed convincing. "It won't. Nobody will hear your name from me. They wouldn't think it, either. They'd just assume I got it from law enforcement sources, or a client."

"And to deliver a warning? What, declaring war on the redneck mafia?" He looked up at me again, and added, "That's not really a thing, and whatever you do, don't call them that."

"I wouldn't." Well, now that he'd warned me, I wouldn't.

"Fine. Fine. But think twice before you go contacting them. Don't use your own phone."

"I don't plan to."

"Fine. Do you have paper and pen?"

I pulled out the tiny metal-cased notebook I always carried and handed it over.

He wrote quickly, handed it back to me.

"Thanks, Eddie. I'll be seeing you soon."

"If you're not dead."

Chapter 45

Ignoring an angry text from Jason to bring the car back right away, I met Susan Kennelly outside the doors of Farrington the next morning. We were buzzed in without comment.

Students swirled by in what, to them, seemed like quiet order. To me it was chaos and noise. How had I ever survived high school? I had never been that young or that loud.

Amy Riordan was at the desk and all smiles for the both of us. I thought her smile for me was a tad warmer than it was for Susan. There was no time for small talk, though, since Dr. Marks came out to usher us into his office immediately.

"I'm glad to hear Gabriel was found quickly," he said, settling behind his desk. "And I want to express my shock and disgust that Dr. Thalheim was tangled up in all this." There was a hint of, not fear, I'd say, but caution in Dr. Marks' bearing that I thought was probably warranted.

"I only want to talk about Gabriel coming back to school," Susan began, cutting straight through all the preliminary dancing I'd expected.

"I'm not entirely sure that's possible," Dr. Marks said.

"Well," I decided to interject, "maybe Ms. Kennelly should come back with a lawyer."

Dr. Marks fixed me with his best imposing stare. I smiled back. I'd had better.

"I'm not entirely clear why you are here, Mr. Dixon," he said.

"He's here because I asked him to be. And while I'm paying him, Dr. Marks, the amount of money he's making *pales* in comparison to what we've spent on Farrington. I would think that should at least create space for discussion."

"Our tuition is scaled appropriately with the legacy and the…"

"I didn't just mean tuition. How many classrooms and buildings on campus have the Kennelly name on them?"

"That is not necessarily germane to the situation."

"Dr. Marks," I said, "how is it you were so courteous on my first visit, and now clearly don't want me here? What changed? The fact that a member of your counseling staff was dealing drugs to students? Or that he was identifying likely suspects for an insurance fraud operation?"

Dr. Marks hid his surprise well but I had him on his heels, for a moment. He recovered quickly, leaning forward over his desk.

"Dr. Thalheim worked under contract with the school from his own psychiatric practice," he began loftily, "he was not fully a member of…"

"But will that explanation wash with the media?"

I could see the headlines running in Dr. Marks' head. *Guidance Counselor, Drug Dealer, Kidnapper* was pretty weak from a prose standpoint but it wouldn't do the school any favors.

"Reporters and lawyers poking around are the last thing Farrington, or its parents, probably want," Susan put in.

"Gabriel filed proper paperwork to drop out of school."

"And he can hardly have been in a right state of mind at the time," I said. "Surely that has to be a factor." Dr. Marks glared at me, though less intently. The instinct to protect the institution was absolutely driving him; that was plain to see. But there were probably better instincts under there somewhere.

"Doctor, I know you need to cover your ass. But I remember our earlier conversation, and I think there's more to you than that. I think you want to do right by the kids here, and that, whatever pressures or influences led Gabriel to do what he did, you *can* find a way to help him get his life back on track. Maybe some kind of medical exemption, and he comes back in the second term. I don't know how this stuff works."

The appeal to his better nature seemed to melt some of that institutional fear away. "Let me look into the possibilities."

"We can discuss them now. Today," Susan said.

"I don't necessarily need to be present for that part," I said. "But there is someone else on campus I'd like to speak with, if I could. Someone who was instrumental in furthering my investigation."

"And who is that person?"

I didn't see how I could work around this one. "Liza Mortimer-Hanes."

Dr. Marks' eyes narrowed. "Should I call her in here?"

"Is it possible to send her a note asking if she's willing to meet with me? I don't want her name over the PA if I can help it."

"How exactly did Ms. Mortimer-Hanes help with the investigation?"

"That's private."

"Not in my school, it isn't."

I sighed. "Dr. Marks, we can sit here and play chicken over who's more stubborn all day, but we've all got busy schedules." Drug-dealers to contact, I thought. Possible gang-wars to initiate. That kind of thing. "And talking to this student is instrumental in state cops and sheriff's deputies and inter-agency anti-opioids taskforces *not* crawling all over your campus in the very near future."

Dr. Marks wrote out a note and went out of his office. I was shooed out and shown to a conference room by Amy.

She took a seat next to me at the table and I glanced at her. She was, as she'd been both times I'd seen her, impeccably made up. She set her hand on my arm.

"Thank you for finding Gabe," she murmured.

"You're…welcome," I said oddly. It seemed a strange thing for her to be thanking me for. And a question immediately formed itself, but I didn't ask it. "It's what I was hired to do."

She nodded. "Everybody's got to pay the bills." She pursed her lips. "The school would like you to sign some paperwork."

I sat up straight, taking my arm out from under her hand. The warm feeling in my chest evaporated.

"Like an NDA?"

"I'm not a lawyer," Amy started, still trying her winning smile. It was very winning. And yet, I did not feel particularly won.

"Neither am I," I said. "And I'm not signing anything unless a lawyer looks at it."

"The school would consider adding to whatever compensation you're receiving."

I went stone faced.

"Considerably."

I was briefly tempted. I usually had enough to pay my bills, small as they were. But large checks were pretty hard to come by for someone who'd quit as many careers as I had.

Amy was still smiling and I liked it less than I ever had.

"Let me ask you a question," I said. "Why do you call Gabriel Gabe?"

She laughed it away. "Why wouldn't I?"

"I'm told he hates it."

She shrugged. "There's hundreds of kids here at Farrington, Mr. Dixon. I can't keep all of that straight."

I did something I shouldn't have done; I compared her to Geneva Lawton. Who had always called Gabriel by his full name. Who'd probably risked her job to call me about Ladders. Whose actions indicated she actually cared about whether I found the kid, whereas Amy Riordan was giving me the impression that she cared a lot more about the institution that signed her checks than the life of a young man.

"I'm definitely not signing anything. Now, if you don't mind, Ms. Riordan, I'd like some privacy."

She withdrew from the room, and I saw the sheaf of papers tucked into her other hand.

A few minutes later, Liza came into the conference room, carrying her bag in front of her like a shield. Her eyes were wide, sockets hollow, cheeks sucked in with worry.

"Are you here to tell me Gabriel's dead or in jail or…"

"Gabriel's fine," I said, "for a certain value of fine."

She deflated so completely and instantly, releasing so much stress that she'd carried, that I was afraid she was going to pass out. She caught herself on a chair and I came around the table to pull it out for her. She waved me away, so I backed around to my seat.

"Is he coming back to school?

"I think his mom is working that out right now. I'm here because I wanted to tell you that the information you provided more or less broke the case."

"Broke is good? From the context clues, broke is good, yes?"

I nodded. Then I said, "However."

She waited. Her face, still tired, gave nothing away. I already liked Liza. I liked her even more now.

"The police would like the names of any students Dr. Thalheim provided with drugs, either illegal or illicit."

"And you told them…"

"That'd I'd go to jail before giving them a name without your consent."

"Really? Why?"

"Because I think most of you would be sheltered from the repercussions of possession, and most of it would come down on Dr. Thalheim. But you never know what somebody out to nail some names to the wall in an investigation might do. And also because I don't think they *need* you to make their case."

"Lots of I think and I don't know in that sentence," Liza said, her eyes suddenly sharp. "Was him giving me Naloxone so wrong, anyway?"

"Dr. Thalheim was neck-deep in some bad s—stuff."

"You can say shit. I'm not a child." She looked like one, and certainly in many important ways she was, but she didn't sound like a kid, and she wasn't acting like one, either. I was even more resolved to keep her out of it if she wanted out of it.

"He was neck-deep in some bad shit. They've got him. But a kid or two under his care on the stand, or at least giving depositions, might make even more certain of it."

She sighed, tapped her fingers on the table. "What would you do?"

I shook my head. "Not about what I would do. It's what you want to do. I'll back you either way."

She took a deep breath. "What if it was just me? No other kids. He didn't give me any illegal drugs."

"He gave them to you in an illegal manner. I'm not sure the law sees a whole lot of difference."

"Not the point. I'll talk to the cops. But I won't give them the names of any other kids."

"I think that's a bold and praiseworthy stance. I think you should get a lawyer before you agree to talk to anyone."

Liza rolled her eyes. "My parents are both lawyers. Before next year is out, my mom will probably be a judge. That won't be a problem."

She was all defiance once again. I pitied the officer who was going to interview Liza and her mother. But only a little.

"One last thing," I said. "You said you wanted to help your friends. That's why the Naloxone. You're the mom around your pals. Yeah?"

"Yeah."

"Well, is that a…career aspiration, or?"

"What are you trying to play counselor now? I'm not sure a guy who dropped out of college should be giving career advice."

"How'd you know that?"

"The internet. You're from Perry Hall, you were supposedly the best high school wrestler Baltimore prep schools had ever seen, you went on a scholarship to…"

I held up a hand. "All right, all right. I'm not offering career advice. It's just…you remind me of a friend of mine. My oldest friend. And she's kinda the same way. Tries to take care of everyone around her, as much as she can. It's part of her career, and I just…" I shrugged. "Maybe you'd benefit from talking to her. Maybe you wouldn't. It's up to you, just like deciding to talk to the cops was up to you. All I'm offering to do is give you her name and her email address."

"Sure," she said with a shrug. I wrote out Dani's email address on a card, made a mental note to bring this up to her, and slid it across the table.

I got up. So did Liza. I gestured toward the door and she stepped out of it, swinging her bag back over her shoulder as she went. I followed her out.

"There's not gonna be an awkward hug situation here," she deadpanned, "is there?"

"Uh. How about a handshake?"

She offered me her hand. I took it. We shook. Her grip was more confident than I imagine most high school boys were.

"Thanks for finding Gabriel," she said, her voice a little smaller.

"I told you I would."

"Yeah," she said, "I'm just not used to believing that kind of bullshit."

"That's fair," I said as I turned back toward the main office. "Just remember, maybe, that it's not *always* bullshit."

"Just usually," she said as I departed.

I decided not to fight for the last word. I was pretty sure I'd lose.

Chapter 46

I had second thoughts every single second of dialing the phone, and talking to the pleasantly neutral voice on the other end. I wasn't surprised when they told me to leave my phone behind. I wasn't sure how they'd feel about what I was bringing them, but that was all the leverage I really had.

That's how I found myself wandering a trailer park behind a Wal-Mart, looking for a number 33. As a kid, I had the disdain for trailer parks taught to those of us lucky enough to grow up in the suburbs. In the years of living in close proximity to these parks I thought I'd overcome that, but I was still ashamed of the classism that put me on edge as I walked around. I lived in a floating goddamn trailer anyway, with less value and less surety than the homes I was walking between. It was dark and shaded, a little muddy. Kids and dogs ran around, played in the evening cool. It felt like a neighborhood.

Finally I found 33. I thought it was the right 33. They hadn't given me a street name, and there was no mailbox outside. I ascended the wooden stairs, expecting them to be rickety. To ricket? They didn't; they were solid and seemed well built. I shook my head to clear the nerves that were making me jittery. I knocked twice and waited.

"It's open."

I walked in, throwing a hand up in front of my eyes. Three car-battery powered flashlights were pointed straight at my eyes the moment I opened the door. Someone brushed past and shut the door behind me.

"Can't be too careful," said a voice from somewhere behind the lights. I had to close my eyes and look at the floor. "Gonna search you."

Which they did, coming up with my wallet, notebook, pocket knife, keys, and a small wad of aluminum foil.

"I thought you weren't coming here to buy," the voice said. I tried to place the accent. It had some of the markers of the county, or the shore, but maybe also Baltimore. "But you got a couple rocks in tinfoil, classic stuff, by the way. We don't move a lot of that, though."

"I'm not here to buy, and those aren't rocks. Just here to pass on a friendly notice."

"About what? You gonna play vigilante? Put on a Punisher t-shirt and buy a rifle?"

"I'm not that stupid," I said. "Just want to give you a heads up about some competition. Not from me."

"Oh?"

"Ever heard of the Aesir MC?"

"The what?"

"A motorcycle club. Call themselves the Aesir. Named after the Norse—"

"Yeah, I know what Aesir means. You're not the only guy in Cecil County ever read a book."

"Well, they're pretty committed to that image. And they're moving into the county from PA."

"How do you know this?"

"Suffice it to say I wrecked something they had going. They shot someone connected to me. Probably gonna shoot me next, they get the chance."

"Why you ain't go to the cops?"

I shrugged. I ventured a look up, but the glare was just too much. "I'm not their favorite guy right now, either."

"What you want, redneck mafia wit-pro?" The three guys in the trailer all shared a chuckle.

"Nope. Just wanted to make you aware."

"Huh. And that's it? Just a warning? Got nothing else?"

"Inside that tinfoil is a SIM card. It's from the burner phone of one of their associates. Guy named Dr. Peter Thalheim. You might read about him in the papers."

"Man, nobody reads the paper anymore. Shit's all online."

"Well, somebody'll cover it there, too. Anyway, that's from the phone he used just to deal with the Aesir."

"Which means what?"

"Which means it's got their phone numbers. Maybe some texts. Maybe some call records. You got a guy who knows what to do with that kinda thing, you can get some useful info from it."

"How about that." A pause. "And this little tidbit ain't gonna cost us anything?"

"Maybe one favor. If any of the numbers on that turn out to be for kids—I mean kids in high school, kids in the area, kids Thalheim was supposed to be looking out for, and instead was selling drugs to, and worse—you don't try and sell them anything."

"Have to discuss that with some associates but seems doable."

"Fine. That's all I wanted."

"Well, fuck off then."

I turned and left. I stumbled down the stairs and leaned against the railing for a minute, till my night vision came back.

I walked back to the car trying to feel like I hadn't just bathed in shit. It didn't work. I wished the case was closed and I'd been paid so I could call Eddie and buy myself something nice. I'd take the *Belle* out into the bay, drop anchor, and smoke myself to the best sleep I knew.

I wished for a lot of things, like a better solution than pitting one batch of criminals against another. I tried to play my job straight. I didn't carry lockpicks. I tried not to carry a weapon. I didn't shake people down and I wasn't purely muscle for hire.

But I'd crossed some kind of line here, and I felt it bone-deep.

I drove back to the *Belle,* had a couple mouthfuls of whiskey for dinner, and tried very hard to sleep.

Chapter 47

Late that night, the buzzing of my phone on the small table next to my bunk pulled me out of a deep sleep. The incoming number wasn't available on caller ID. I swallowed hard and flicked to accept it.

"Jack Dixon." My voice sounded like a quarter ton of gravel had just been blown through my esophagus.

"Wake up call, Mr. Dixon," the voice on the other end said. "The info you gave us came good. Gonna need you to clear some things up, though."

"What the fuck are you talking about?"

"Mr. Dixon. You got an hour to be at the following location." He then rattled off a series of what I soon realized were coordinates—latitude and longitude.

"Hang on. Let me get some paper and copy this down." I was awake now, for sure. My heart thudded in my chest, filled up my ears. A chill was working its way up from my stomach.

I dutifully wrote down the coordinates and then that charming, cold, neutral voice on the other end repeated that I had one hour and disappeared.

I got dressed in jeans and a dark blue Henley. I considered arming myself; I had some knives lying around. The brass knuckles were still in the company car. In the end I decided on those, as I liked my metal encased right hook a lot better than I did my odds with a sharp kitchen knife.

Besides, I couldn't afford to ruin any of my good knives on some biker's ribs.

I was in the car and headed north inside ten minutes, but not until I pulled loose the tell-tale meter plugged into the car's electronics that read its mileage and where it had traveled. According to the GPS, I wasn't going far; within the county, but up near the PA line. I kept the windows rolled down in hopes that the night air would help me wake up.

Frankly the mystery of where I was going and what I was meant to do there was plenty in that regard.

To get to the location eventually required turning off a paved road a while after I'd passed a Scout Reservation. I worried that I was beating the hell out of the undercarriage of the firm's car as I rode up a badly rutted dirt road. I know I smacked the thing against the ground at least a couple of times.

Eventually the road ran out, and GPS told me I had one tenth of a mile to go. I suddenly got a text.

Looks like you're walking from there. When you get beyond the trees, do not run.

A second text came in just moments later.

Do not run.

I killed the engine, stuffed the keys into a pocket, and started walking. The feeble light of my phone did not do much to illuminate my path so I got my Maglite out and clicked it on. A stand of trees ahead of me, a field and a whole lot of blackness beyond that.

I cleared the trees, shut my phone off, and slipped the knuckles on to my right hand. I kept the Maglite in my left. The instinct to sweep it around the field was overpowering, but I resisted.

Then suddenly, on the far end of the field, lights came alive. Engines roared.

Three motorcycles bounded across the field toward me. I turned to dive back into the cover of the trees, prepared to leg it for the car.

The inarguable insistence of the text I'd gotten kept me rooted in place, doing the dumbest thing possible: nothing.

By the time I'd gathered myself it was too late anyway. The bikers could certainly have given chase if I'd tried to go then.

They didn't circle me. That, at least, was something. I could pick a direction and run if I had to. They pulled up a few yards away.

The rumble of the engines subsided; silhouettes detached themselves and advanced on me.

"Mr. Dixon. A liar and a coward," one of them — the one in the middle, the shortest and broadest of the three — said. I couldn't make out too many details since I'd killed my Maglite's beam, but all were bearded. I could hear the creak of leather, smell oil and metal, hear the tromp of heavy boots in the grass.

I could also see the outline of one of them drawing a weapon — a shotgun, sawed off, wildly illegal — from a drop holster on his thigh.

The stocky one, the talker, came forward till the ambient light of the stars helped me make out his features. Not Troy, certainly; this fellow was at least a foot smaller. I heard the whisper of a knife leave its sheath.

Not quite time yet to make a play, I thought. But nearly so. I tried to stay loose, to breathe easy.

"You broke your word, Mr. Dixon. Then you tried to sell us out to some local movers, I understand. They would rather reach an accommodation with us than start some pointless war over turf. Surely it will come to that some day, but there may be years of fruitful interaction now that they've given us a peace offering."

He raised the seax. Starlight glinted off the blade.

"Are you going to cooperate, or will I take more than an ear to start?"

"Nah," I said, trying to project a confidence I did not feel.

"It was not a yes or n…"

He didn't finish the question, because then I came alongside his face with the knuckles. Hitting with my fist wrapped in them hurt.

Him, more than me.

I heard bone crunch and I knew I'd broken his jaw. I was never going to get away from the one with the shotgun. But I wasn't going to eat two barrels of buckshot while sitting on my thumb.

Then the gunshots rang out. They were the crack of high-powered rifles, not the full-throated roar of a shotgun.

I dove forward, away from the falling biker I'd decked, seeking the cover of the bikes. The one whose jaw I'd broken had staggered back to his feet and taken a pistol from his belt. Tough bastard, I'd give him that. But another rifle shot dropped him and he lay just a couple of feet from me, his face a ruin of shredded flesh and blood.

There were a few more shots. Not many. Probably less than a dozen, all told. By the time they were done, all three of the bikers lay still and unmoving on the ground.

I continued to lay still between the bikes. I only got up as I heard footsteps crunching over the grass. I thought about grabbing one of the biker's weapons—I kicked the heavy bladed knife as I stood up—but I thought better of it.

By the time I'd stood and picked my way around the bodies, they'd closed in. Four of them, covering every direction I could go.

"Relax, Dixon. You gave us a good tip." The one doing the talking was, I was pretty certain, the same one I'd talked to on the phone. Maybe the one I'd talked to in the trailer. They were all indistinct shapes with long rifles in their hands, straps trailing beneath them. And they wore hunting getups, probably camouflage, including balaclavas that hid everything but an oval of skin around the eyes.

Even in broad daylight, I wouldn't have been able to ID any of them.

"Why the hell did you bring me out here?"

The leader lifted his rifle and tapped my chest with the barrel.

It was a tad warm.

"Mind your tone, prep-school boy," he said. "Now you know you ain't dealing with amateurs. Nice punch, by the way. Hell, I think you broke that fucker's jaw," he said. There was some laughter around him. He didn't laugh; neither did I.

"You were at the scene of a multiple killing. With a weapon in your hand, that's been used. A competent cop could probably put that together if they got a tip. Just lookin' out for you."

The muzzle of the rifle continued to rest lightly on my chest. I did not like how it felt.

If it was just me and him—maybe just me, him, and one other guy—I would've taken my chances. I was pretty sure I could grab the gun with my left and pull him into a punch with my metal-wrapped right fist.

But that would've done me no good when there were three other guns that, while not pointed at me currently, could be course corrected in a matter of moments.

"Okay," I said, and even I heard my voice crack a little, "what now?"

"You go the fuck home and forget the Aesir existed. Not your problem anymore."

I didn't give them the satisfaction of running back to my car, no matter how badly I wanted to.

Chapter 48

I tried to sleep, until I finally gave up while lying awake at five-thirty a.m. I got up, chewed on a tasteless apple, swallowed some tasteless almond butter. I even took a mouthful of whiskey, which I never did first thing in the morning. But I wound up merely swishing it around my mouth before spitting it over the starboard side.

I untied the boat and went for a short cruise. I got out the 'novelty paperweight' and scrubbed it down with bleach and water and vinegar. When I was well out on the water, I threw the brass knuckles out into the river, hoping like hell that the current would be kind to a sailor, and carry it to the Chesapeake, or the Atlantic beyond, and away from any place with detectives and crime labs and search warrants. I thought about throwing my clothes in after it, but from what I could tell, they had escaped all stains other than mud.

I got back to the marina around the time I'd usually get up, a little before nine. I went to the gym and did everything I could do: too many dumb-bells and too much cardio, but I was keeping my hand in. I tried not to hear gunshots, the sound of bodies hitting the ground, or the rasp of that knife coming out of its sheath while I worked.

Then I drove the car up to the firm. I tried to sneak in, drop the keys, and bolt. But somebody was watching for me and I immediately heard a yell from the management corridor.

"DIXON. GET IN HERE."

I sighed, steeled myself, and wondered if I was about to be looking for a job.

I marched in. Jason looked stern, but not quite in a firing mood. I'd thought that before, about bosses. I'd been wrong.

"Where the hell do you think you were going? Why didn't you bring that car back yesterday?"

"One," I said, holding up a finger, "there's this phenomenon I call the Peasant's Instinct, which indicates that the *less* time one spends around authority figures, the better. That the potential negative consequences…"

"Less bullshit."

"Fine. I needed the car yesterday. Wrap-up on the Kennelly case." Watching a gang war start. Being part of the set up to an execution. That kind of thing.

"Good. From now on, company cars are barred to you. I'm dropping you from the list of approved drivers with the fleet insurance."

"How the hell am I gonna do…"

"Your job? Buy a damn car. And that brings me to my second point."

He produced two envelopes from his desk, and handed them over. Both had my name written on them.

"Ms. Kennelly paid up last night. In full, and then some. She didn't even blink at the expense report."

"I didn't submit one."

"Brock did. I did. Don't worry, I didn't bilk her. I just estimated what you were likely to have spent on gas, tolls, ammo, food, and stupidity tax."

The first envelope had the firm livery on it and my name in the address window. The second was addressed to me, care of the firm. The return address was ADI Holdings.

I opened it with a thumb. Inside was a slim letter wrapped around a check. Mindful of etiquette and many a childhood admonition to read the card before looking at the money, I read. The handwriting was a little spidery.

Mr. Dixon,

Though affairs at present prevent me from being as involved in my son's life as I might like, I nevertheless retain a father's gratitude for the safe return of his son. Below is a token of that gratitude. It also contains an apology for your treatment at the hands of my employees. They are sometimes overzealous in what they perceive as the protection of my interests.

Best,

Thomas Kennelly

The check slipped to the floor as I scanned the letter. I picked it up. I blinked at it several times.

"May I see it?"

I held it out to Jason, but I did not let him touch it.

"That is considerable gratitude," he said.

"Yep."

"Go buy a car."

"Let's not be hasty."

"There's an auto auction every week down in Bel Air. Seized property and the like. *Go buy a car.*"

"Fine, fine," I said. I'd already given up enough of myself the night before, why not submit to the car, too? "Look, I promised to make a friend dinner tonight, and she'll actually kill me if I don't deliver."

Jason nodded at the checks in my hands. "You've got carfare."

"Fine. I'll file a final report tomorrow."

"Good. Get out of here. And Jack," Jason said, "try to be just a little bit more of a team player. Like, eleven percent more. And don't get any of your co-workers shot again, or I'll fire you."

"What if I get myself shot?"

"That I could live with."

"Noted." I left his office with a sarcastic salute. I almost stopped and asked for a company gun, but if I suddenly started packing without complaint, Jason would know something was wrong.

I used my phone to immediately deposit the first check, the one from Ms. Kennelly. The second would've put me over the monthly limit on mobile deposits, so the first stop with my Lyft was the bank.

Chapter 49

Buying the supplies to make the Beef Wellington Dani had requested certainly put a dent in my suddenly flush checking account. It would've paid for several weeks' worth of nut butter, carrots, and apples. Not to mention the occasional lunch salad or the absolute extravagance of a burger for dinner.

I texted Dani as I shopped, asking about veg, sides, and starters.

Fuck vegetables, she replied. *Potatoes. Em is handling cheese and crackers.*

I added a five-pound bag of Yukon golds and an extra half pound of Normandy butter.

It was a long Lyft ride back from Janssen's in Wilmington to Dani and Emily's house just on the Cecil County side of the Susquehanna, but I had the money. And Jason had been right to take away my right to drive a company car.

Frankly, that was less of a punishment than I probably deserved. On the drive I alternated between closing parts of the case file I'd built and looking for info on the auction at which I'd been instructed to purchase a car. It was slim pickings, mostly hatchbacks and coupes that had probably been seized from hapless kids carrying a trace of weed in their glove box.

I tried to put my mind in a happier place by making the reservation for Saturday's date with Geneva Lawton, and perusing the menu. I tended to navigate the menu several days in advance of attendance at any good restaurant so I knew how to adjust what I ate in the days leading up to it. And it gave me something to look forward to. There was a good chance I was getting crab cakes with shrimp and salmon mousse if they were on; shrimp and grits was in with a chance, though.

This got me through the long ride, and the expense of it, without succumbing to the mood that was trying to drag me in. I was in the act of knocking on the door of a nice split-level ranch at the end of a cul-de-sac when it opened from the inside. That threw me off balance, and I almost dropped the two shopping bags I was carrying. But through superior body-control and a keen awareness of how much it had all cost, I kept it under control.

Emily was about as different from Dani as it was possible to be. Shorter, curvier, prone to pin-up hairstyles and tasteful makeup. She had a cheese knife in her hand and a yellow apron on over a pale green dress. "You know where the kitchen is," she said, pointing with the cheese knife. Indeed I did, and I unloaded everything on the kitchen table and the island.

Once my hands were free, I was suddenly wrapped in a hug. At least until I let out an "Oof" and Emily let go and stepped back.

"Sorry," she said, "I forgot about your ribs." She looked speculatively at my face. "You've looked better," she said, pointing at the fading bruise under my eye. "Are you eating," she added, suddenly tapping the cheese knife against my chest. Despite the presence of a blade against my shirt, I did not feel threatened.

"Yes."

"Anything other than peanut butter and whiskey?"

I froze for a second too long. "Carrots."

She let out an exasperated sigh. "The world punishes us enough, Jack. You don't have to do it yourself."

I shrugged. She'd always been able to see through me. "Only discipline I know, Em."

"Fine, fine. At least let me pour you a glass of wine."

"That I will not argue with."

Soon enough I had my sleeves rolled up, a red apron on—Emily had tried to give me pink, but I submitted to toxic masculinity and refused—and a puff pastry mixing with the dough hook in a bowl. Dani got home by the time I was putting it in the fridge.

The rest of the afternoon passed pleasantly. I finished the pastry. I made mushroom duxelles with shallot. I peeled the potatoes against my usual protocol for mashing them, because when I suggested simply rinsing them off, Dani had glared at me.

It took hours, but they were *good* hours. I couldn't have done this every night—the home, the closeness, the wine. It would've driven me crazy. But it was nice to forget about drugs, drug dealers, bikers, threats on my life, and counting every single calorie. I didn't think about gunshots, dead bodies, or gang wars for upwards of an hour at a time.

The wine helped with that. I started worrying about the calories with the second glass and began entering them into an app on my phone. Dani glared at me again, refilled my glass, and took away my phone. It was about then that the constructed Wellingtons—lightly seared tenderloin, slathered with Dijon, wrapped in prosciutto and duxelles and then a homemade crepe, then the puff pastry—went in the oven.

"Why'd you only make two," Dani asked when she saw the sheet go in the oven.

"Would you look at how clean this thing is," I said, tapping a finger on the gleaming gas stove. "You could just eat straight off of it."

"Jack, you didn't think you were going to make us dinner and then *leave* did you?"

"It's…kinda how I was operating."

"Well, it ain't happening," Dani said, tapping me in the chest with one sharp finger. "Those monsters can each feed three people, and you're going to be one of them."

I didn't fight too hard about it. I demurred when Emily asked about the cost of the groceries as we ate.

"Nice to cook for other people. Those muscles'll atrophy, I don't use 'em once in a while."

"So will these," Dani said, poking my arm. "You been in the gym? I'll check with Nick. It was me who sicced him on you."

"Why'd you do that? Don't like him?"

"No," Dani said. "I like him just fine, and I wanted to make sure you weren't hurting yourself."

"Plenty of other folks lined up to do that," I said. "And I *have* been in the gym. But there's the matter of a wrenched-up back and bruised, possibly broken ribs holding me back a little."

"Dumb-bell comp…"

"Dumb-bell complexes and cardio. I know. I've been doing that. I won't try to lift anything heavy until next week at the earliest."

"Enough with the gym talk," Emily declared. Neither of us were going to argue with her.

"You wrap up whatever case you were working on?"

"Mostly. Just paperwork and closure meetings now. And uh, I wanted to ask you something about that, Dani."

She set her fork down as she savored a bite of Wellington. The food on her plate had been as carefully cross sectioned into perfect pieces as if she'd been performing surgery on it.

"Is this another favor?"

"Might be."

"Is it to do with an email I got out of the blue from some high school kid?"

"Ah," I said. "Liza is not the shy and retiring type."

"Why'd you give her my address?"

"Because she reminded me of you," I said. "She's her class mom. Trying to protect people, take care of them, but in ways that were gonna get her in trouble eventually."

"Explain," she and Em said together. So I did, telling her about running into the kid at the party-barn and the drugs she was carrying.

"Lot of coincidence in this work of yours," Emily said.

"I prefer to think of it as being open to the whims of the universe," I said, only realizing how dumb it sounded when it was out of my mouth. We all laughed, though the two of them went first.

"Anyway," I said, "this girl's gonna keep looking for ways to be proactive about protecting the people around her, and I thought, gee, who do I know like that?"

This time Emily laughed, I joined her, and Dani grimaced.

"You don't have to become the girl's mentor," I said. "Just seemed like there's something in her that's an awful lot like something in you.

"Kid need a way to pay for college? I could help with ROTC scholarships."

"I think her parents could probably buy a small liberal arts school," I said. "But that's the sort of thing that might appeal to her, if she thought it was her own idea."

"Fine. I'll take the girl's emails. Can we get on with dinner? And what'd you make for dessert?"

I froze, wine glass halfway to the table. More laughter.

It was the best night I'd had in ages, and it ended in Dani getting out a bottle of Springbank Ten, and me sleeping in their spare room.

Chapter 50

I slept that night in the absolute extravagance of a full-size bed. I did not, as far as I could recall, dream of bikers, knives, or gunshots. I did wake up with an unusual weight on my chest. I looked up to see an impossibly large orange cat sleeping on my chest. He had a huge ruff of fur around his neck, hiding the collar he wore.

"Hey, Gimli," I muttered. I sat up cautiously, petting Dani and Emily's cat, who immediately started playfully gnawing on the bones of my wrist. I am certain it was playful because he probably could have bitten at least a finger off if he had a mind to. I cautiously moved my head around on my neck, took some deep breaths.

No signs of a hangover. No missed calls or voicemails. Seemed like a good day to take off, read, maybe give the *Belle* a thorough cleaning. Dani and Emily were both gone, and had left a travel mug full of coffee next to the boxes with my sparkling clean knives, and small bag of other tools—favorite spatulas and such. There was also a spare set of keys and a note in Emily's fine, slanted handwriting.

It simply said *Anytime.*

I used the keys to lock the door behind me, hid them in a plant, and texted Dani to thank her and tell her where I'd put them.

I hailed a cab and was in the process of giving the *Belle* the stem to stern interior cleaning she deserved when Ms. Kennelly called, asking me if I'd talk with Gabriel.

I said sure, which is how I found myself at their house just a couple of hours later. The kid was folded awkwardly on the couch, wrapped in a blanket. He looked a little dazed, and was probably either lightly medicated or wanted to be. I took a chair opposite him and watched as he flicked channels. Susan stood by a little awkwardly, leaning against the chair I sat in.

"What'd you want to talk about, Gabriel?"

He put the remote down and looked at me. Making eye contact was difficult for him.

"I wanted to thank you," he said. "For finding me. My mom says you got hurt doing it."

I waved that away. "Pain heals. And I'm still not sure what that had to do with your case."

"It's because his father is a paranoiac," Susan muttered behind me.

I decided to try and pull the conversation away from that. "You, uh, decided what you're gonna do yet?"

He nodded. "In a couple more weeks I go back. Audit classes this semester, then take them again next semester. I can still finish and graduate in the summer."

I nodded. "Gonna go back to running?"

He shrugged. "Why?"

"Heard you were good at it."

That brought the eye contact. "Just 'cause you're good at something doesn't mean you like it."

"I know how that is."

He sat up straighter. "Do you?"

I nodded.

"What was it for you?"

"Wrestling."

"What, high school?"

"And college, on a scholarship. Big Ten," I said. "Hated every second of it."

"But you kept doing it?"

I shook my head. "Nope. Quit my sophomore year."

He smiled. "How'd that feel?"

"Felt great. For about five minutes," I said. "Then I realized I had no other way to pay for college and they weren't gonna keep me around out of the goodness of their hearts." I realized this particular part of the story maybe didn't track for Gabriel. His father could certainly pay for college, if the check I'd gotten yesterday was any indication.

"What'd you do?"

"I literally ran away and joined the Navy." He laughed weakly. "I don't really recommend that particular method."

"So what would you do? Go back and rejoin cross-country?"

Why did everyone keep asking my advice? I was the biggest screwup I knew.

"I'd talk to my friends, and my mom, and my pastor or priest or chaplain or guru, if I had one. I'd especially talk to a friend like Liza, who was as worried about you as I think she ever has been about anything. And then I'd see what I felt, and whether it was worth keeping it in my life. You stop doing a thing that suddenly, you might find a hole in your days where it used to be." I wasn't sure what I was saying, but the kid was listening.

"Running was why I took some pills in the first place."

I leaned forward. "Eh?"

"It hurt, you know. Running that much. And I never got a moment's rest from it. Just…coaches always in my ears, letters from colleges, texts. Nobody asked if I wanted to run, they just kept throwing the uniform at me, telling me to eat, telling me to get in the gym, telling me to get to practice."

"Look, if you want me to go shake down your coaches, I can do that, but…"

Thankfully they both recognized the joke. "That all sounds miserable," I went on. "And a lot of folks will tell you misery builds character, teaches you who you are."

"What do you think?"

I thought I certainly lived like I believed that, because I'd heard it all my life. I didn't think it was what Gabriel wanted to hear.

"Tell a coach to fuck off once in a while."

Gabriel laughed. Susan tried to shoot me a dirty look but she was trying too hard not to laugh to really sell it. "Really, though, tell a coach to back off. Take some time to be a kid. Do something that you want to do, whether that's reading or napping or playing a video game. There's a difference between discipline and misery. You can have one without the other." Or so they told me. I had rarely handed anyone as big a raft of bullshit as I was currently unspooling for the kid. At least, judged in terms of how *I* lived.

Gabriel nodded. "Maybe I'll go back for track."

"Always your call, kid."

He cracked a yawn and I glanced up at his mom, who frowned.

"I, uh, should probably get out of your hair." Handshakes with both of them, and I was out the door. Susan had tried to press a twenty on me for a car, but I demurred.

I left pondering if I was going to ever take my own advice, which I realized was almost exactly what Emily had said to me the night before.

Chapter 51

Saturday morning I went to the gym and did absolutely as much as I could get away with for the third time in four days. Swallowing no small amount of self-loathing, I even used a curl bar. I looked longingly at the squat racks. I might even have walked over and tapped one, promising I'd be back soon.

Then it was off to the barbershop. It had been a few weeks. My hair fell away from the clippers in a curtain of light brown, or dark blond, depending on the lighting and angle, I guess. I'd never really decided what color it was. I even had him trim and shape my beard, putting it nice and neat against my face, and shave my neck and sides with the razor.

Then I went back to the *Belle* and used a beard brush and a wet rag to wash away any remnants of the haircut from my neck and chest. The last thing I needed was the distraction of an itch. I started wondering if this was really a date.

"Sure it is," I said aloud.

But what if it isn't?

"She used the word," I muttered. "And anyway, I'm not going to spend all day worrying about it."

Saying that aloud didn't mean I was going to do it, though. I did spend most of the afternoon reading, before finally deciding to *officially* get ready. I considered my shirts, and decided on the only currently intact button down I had on the boat, a kind of soft green. I might have called it sage if I was feeling fanciful. Jeans. Shoes were going to be a bit tougher. My black Converse were far too sweat-stained. My running shoes were a mess. I looked at the still mud-stained dress shoes I'd worn when tussling with the two security goons in the park.

I got out the shoe polish kit and went to work.

Dressed, freshly shorn and shaved, and wearing a judicious application of Club Man Bay Rum, I ordered a ride and went to pace in the parking lot and wait for it.

* * *

"You look stunning." I felt like I blurted the words out when I met Gen in front of the restaurant, but they were true. She was. She wore a blue sundress that left her shoulders bare for the lingering heat. Her hair was swept back as usual, she wore very little in the way of jewelry—just small gold earrings.

"Thank you," she said, and I thought there was just the hint of a flush under her tan cheeks. "You clean up nice yourself." I held the door for her, and she squeezed my hand at the hostess stand. I stopped wondering if this was a date.

When we were seated with cocktails—we both ordered the one with gin, basil syrup, lemon, and club soda—we started the various conversational feints.

"So, your boss sent me a letter."

She held up a hand. "I'd rather not talk about work. It's Saturday."

"No problem. What would you like to talk about?"

From there, we traded back and forth. She was from Elkton; dad worked on county maintenance, mom ran a day care, and she'd had to pay for her own education after high school. She would finish the MBA at UD in the spring and wasn't sure what came next. Maybe law school, maybe looking for a bigger job at one of the Wilmington firms.

"I don't much like working for ADI, at least not just sitting at the desk," she said, "and I know I said I didn't want to talk about work. But it paid for college and grad school, up front. Not even reimbursement. Not a lot of places'll do that."

I had to admit that was fair. I also had to reveal my own side of things, like dropping out of a Big Ten school on a wrestling scholarship and joining the Navy.

"Had you always wanted to be a sailor?"

"Not even a little bit," I admitted. "But I was going to get kicked out of school at the end of the semester when the bill came due, and I walked past a recruiter's office. It wouldn't involve going home."

"So you let an impulse decide the next four years of your life?"

"Pretty much," I admitted. "But at least the Navy taught me to cook."

She leaned forward over her plate — she'd ordered scallops, me the crab cakes, after we split an appetizer of Brussels sprouts with chili oil and aioli — and said, "You can cook?"

"I can feed two or two hundred, so long as I've got the ingredients, tools, and space."

"Going to have to test that."

"Name the time and place."

She smiled. We ate. We liked some of the same music; she had a more modern and indie-inclusive view, but we shared a certain respect for some of the American masters: Prine, Clark, Raitt, Emmy Lou. She made me promise to listen to a band called First Aid Kit, and another called Lake Street Dive. I probably would've promised her just about anything after my second gin cocktail.

By the time dinner was over, and she'd ordered dessert and me a whiskey, it had been going so well I'd forgotten everything but the table and the woman sitting across from me.

I walked her to her car, lightly holding hands.

"So, when can I prove to you I can cook?"

"Next week?"

"Sounds good." I started to lean down. She beat me to it.

I floated home with some Prine lyrics in my head, from "Long Monday." The part about a kiss that'll last all week. I'd done my best. I think she had, too.

All in all that beating I got last week was looking like my best luck in a long time.

* * *

I had that floating feeling as I walked down the dock to the *Belle*. I could've danced, done one of those jump in the air and click your heel numbers. I went inside, poured myself a Manhattan, and started looking for something to read. I walked into my bunk, rummaging through the rows and stacks of books on the little-used kitchen table. And it was only then that I saw it.

It took me a moment to register it atop the blanket, just in front of the pillows. I leaned in close, turned to my box of work gear and got my Maglite. I clicked it on, leaned back in close, and examined what had been left on my pillow.

A bird skull. A raven's, I'd bet. And with my initials carved delicately into the side.

The warm elation of a successful first date turned sour and cold at record speed.

Chapter 52

For the next several days, I never put the *Belle* in at the same place. Overnight I docked out in a channel, or back at the Landing, or sometimes out in the middle of fucking nowhere. I slept well, at least, courtesy of a visit to Eddie and my newly improved finances.

Every day I was a dutiful employee, showing up to do whatever office work Jason wanted, catching rides other office drones or via Lyft. For once, I liked the idea of having other people—some of them armed—around me for most of the light hours of the day.

Finally, the time came for the auto auction, and I found myself down in Bel Air. Bob drove me, since there were some vehicles from his department going on the block.

"You're gonna look for something sensible, right?"

"Bob," I said calmly, "I am being forced into a lifestyle change that I don't want and can't afford. Please do not rub it in by pushing me into a goddamn hatchback."

"Just don't go getting stars in your eyes over some convertible or sportscar."

"Death. First."

"Are you going to take this seriously?"

"Only as seriously as it needs to be. I need to get from point A to point B. Occasionally to grocery shop. I'll be fine."

He let it go.

We got to the auction. I drifted between the lanes. I threw a half-hearted bid out on a Prius but quickly lost track of it.

I was a mixture of giddiness over last week's date with Gen and terror over the raven's skull that had been left on my pillow. Even without that kind of turmoil, this whole directive to buy a car felt wrong. Who was my boss to dictate how I lived?

He was the man who'd fire me if I didn't come up with reliable transportation, that's what. I drifted away from the lane I'd been monitoring, the one Bob had directed me to.

And then I saw It.

My eyes landed on the hunter green frame from a dozen yards away. I practically sprinted over and entered the bidding as soon as it started. It cost more than I meant to spend, and by the time I'd won, I wasn't sure exactly what had happened until me and Bob were standing beside It after I had handed over the largest stack of cash I'd ever held in my hand.

"Jack."

"Yes, Bob."

"Do you have a license for this?"

"Nope."

"Do you know how to ride It?"

"Nope."

"Did you think this through?"

"Do I ever?"

He sighed. "We'll arrange for it to be held. I'll borrow a trailer and haul it down."

I stood there stroking the gas tank and saddle of my slightly used, seized-property 2015 Indian Scout. I tentatively sat on it. My feet found the pedals, my hands the bars.

It sure felt a hell of a lot better than a hatchback.

* * *

Bob was true to his word and the next afternoon I heard the rumble of his truck. From the deck I could see him wrangling the trailer with It strapped in place.

I came out to meet him. He got out of the truck, his face a mask of anger. He held a newspaper and a file folder in his hand.

"Inside the goddamn boat," he said through clenched teeth.

Baffled, I followed him.

Once we were on the *Belle* I walked straight into a punch that, if he hadn't pulled it a little, could probably have broken my jaw. Then he threw the paper at me as I lay on the deck, dazed.

"What the fuck, Bob?"

"Just look," he hissed.

I picked up the paper and saw the headline. "BIKER BODIES FOUND." I scanned the story; gangland style stuff, ambush, shoot-out. A lot of words were tossed around. The one that stood out was Aesir.

I knew the bodies. Of course I did. I'd seen them die.

I absolutely could not tell Bob Sanderson that.

"So why did this get me hit?"

"You do it?"

"Jesus, Bob. Since when am I some kind of gun-hand, can shoot down three bikers before they get a shot off?"

"Oh, they got a shot off. Two or three. But it was pretty professional stuff. It was a fucking shooting gallery just our side of the PA line. So I'm gonna ask you again. You do it?"

"The only firearms I have any access to are secured in the firm's gun locker. You're welcome to go check them and count the ammo inventory. Every round has to be accounted for."

"You don't have a piece around here?"

"I don't like guns and I won't have one on my boat." I was beginning to think about changing my mind on that score, but I hadn't quite yet. I thought maybe the local boys were giving the Aesir as much as they could handle.

"Well," Bob said, "you better hope that between these three and the couple we have in custody that the Aesir numbers are *depleted*." He held the file folder out. I came to my feet and flipped it open.

I almost dropped it immediately when I saw the crime scene photos.

"This one is up in PA. We were alerted to it because the LEOs there suspect the Aesir, and the dead guy is from Cecil County." Bob droned on about the guy's record. I didn't hear him; I just stared at the photos.

A man had been tied face down in a field, had his ribs cut away from his spine, and his lungs pulled out over his shoulders. I felt acid rising up my throat.

Bob had stopped talking. I looked up at him. I knew I was pale.

"That's a Blood Eagle," I said.

"A what?"

I closed the folder, took a deep breath, then tapped it with one finger. "What they did to this guy. It's from Viking sagas. May or may not have been a real thing in Viking days."

"Looks pretty fucking real now."

"Yeah." He took the proffered folder. I felt weak. "Got something to show you."

Anger dropped. Cop inquisitiveness replaced it. "What?"

I rummaged in a cabinet and brought out the raven skull. I'd sealed it in a plastic bag. The J and D carved in stood out in the morning light. Bob looked at it curiously. "Should've brought this to the cops."

"Yeah, well. Protective custody ain't really my style." I paused. "Are you really in the throes of grief that three outlaw bikers and one drug dealer have eaten it?"

He looked up from the skull. "The way you ask that makes me think you did have something to do with it."

"Test my hands for residue if you want."

He frowned, shook his head. "Come help me get this ridiculous motorcycle off my trailer."

We went outside and carefully unstrapped It, muscled it down into an empty parking spot close to my slip.

Bob handed me some pamphlets about motorcycle training courses and licensing, and opened the driver side of his truck. Then he turned and looked at me.

"You're right, Jack. I'm not real sorry that some bikers died in a field just because it's in my county. But if you started a gang war? The bodies that start dropping are on *you*." He got in, the engine revved, and he drove away.

I took a look at the Scout, thumbed through the material, and decided to spend at least the following hour not thinking about how many bodies would end up on my books when all was said and done.

The End

Jack Dixon will return in **CHEAP HEAT**

About the author

Daniel M. Ford is the author of *The Paladin Trilogy*. A native of Baltimore, he has an M.A. in Irish Literature from Boston College and an M.F.A. in Creative Writing from George Mason University. He teaches English at a college prep high school in rural Maryland.

Find him on Twitter @soundingline.

Coming Soon

Jack Dixon takes his PI talents on the road when a pro wrestler's outlandish Civil War-themed act results in death threats. Jack accompanies the self-styled "U.S. Grant—an old college buddy—and his regional wrestling promotion on their fall tour in hopes of sniffing out the mystery and escaping his troubled past...and to avoid any more harrowing run-ins with the deadly Aesir gang. Struggling with a budding romance, the specter of his college-era mistakes, and the undercurrents of a fanatic pro wrestling fandom, some of whom may just be willing to kill, Jack soon finds himself dragged into the limelight—and squarely into the crosshairs of his most dangerous enemies.

About Santa Fe Writers Project

SFWP is an independent press dedicated to the craft of writing. We publish exciting fiction and creative nonfiction of every genre, maintain an online literary journal, and run an annual internationally-recognized Awards Program.

Find us on Facebook, Twitter @sfwp, and at sfwp.com